A Dying in the Night

A Dying
in the Night

JAN ROFFMAN

PUBLISHED FOR THE CRIME CLUB BY

DOUBLEDAY & COMPANY, INC.

GARDEN CITY, NEW YORK

1974

All of the characters in this book
are fictitious, and any resemblance
to actual persons, living or dead,
is purely coincidental.

ISBN: 0-385-07197-3

Library of Congress Catalog Card Number 73–83665
Copyright © 1974 by Doubleday & Company, Inc.
All Rights Reserved
Printed in the United States of America

First Edition

A Dying in the Night

ONE

As Elaine closed the front door her mind, recently released from sleep, operated simultaneously on two levels. The upper circuit noted it was Sunday, the second in September, the sun wanly autumnal, the trees that lined and overhung the road stripped of the first percentage of their leaves by the gale that had ravaged them during the night. The Corby children, boisterous and contentious, were being coerced into a minibus by their overtense, strident-voiced mother and long-suffering father. Mrs Marsden, hatted, gloved, dark-coated, was off to early Mass, so ostentatiously devout she barely raised an eyelid in greeting.

The lower level of awareness was conscious of labyrinthian memory tunnels storing a quarter of a century of time devoured since, at the age of five, she'd made the first of her uncountable visits to No. 8 Hartfield Road: as a skipping, carefree child, as a girl wholly possessed by love, and now as a woman of thirty, communication between the two homes reduced to a single strand between herself and a crippled old man. For a second she stood motionless, totally obsessed by the dead and the lost, a sense more poignant than bereavement in that it was a state of permanent aloneness in a world of the living from which there was no reprieve.

As, somewhere near at hand, eight o'clock struck, the present displaced the past and her steps automatically quickened. Elaine Lowther was lightly built, her best feature the lustrous fawn hair which she wore in a simple page-boy style that framed her oval, pale-skinned face. Her mouth was, maybe for some tastes, too wide, but it fell naturally into a smile that either warmed or stimulated confidence in its recipient. Only her heavy-lidded grey eyes that were apt, unless her attention was fully engaged, to be set in a trancelike immobility, hinted that Elaine Lowther had at her disposal some secret limbo of retreat; contrarily, when she was at ease, they were curiously innocent eyes for a woman of thirty.

On working days she made Mr Ellis's morning tea at seven; on Saturdays and Sundays, at his insistence, she did not cross the road until eight. He was always awake and waiting for her, his glance focused on the door, his reply to her cry: "Hello, Mr Ellis," waiting on his tongue.

As she called out, she automatically looked into the letter box—although there was no postal delivery on Sunday —not in hope, but out of an ingrained habit she could not cure. Made deaf for a moment, she missed Mr Ellis's answer. Or had he, perhaps, for once overslept?

She opened the door into the dining room that, since arthritis had locked Mervyn Ellis's joints, had been converted into a downstairs bedroom, and as though illuminated by sheet lightning every detail of the horrific scene photographed itself on her mind; yet, paradoxically, was instantly rejected because what sight reported to her brain could be no more than a nightmare of horrendous proportions. The smashed skull, the broken, stiffening hand flung in a futile gesture of protection across his face. The blood sprayed on the wall and the floor, gouts of it already darkening from red to brown. The French window, one pane smashed, flying open, allowing the slackening wind to play with the loose sheets of an evening paper and the sleeve of a shirt hung over a chair.

Her left foot moved one pace forward, then retreated. She recognised death, knew no heart could stir in that brutally assaulted body, no breath move between lips that were stretched in a rictus of terror. The shivering mounted from the soles of her feet, gathered momentum until her whole body seemed racked by ague, the only sound in the room that had witnessed violent death that of her teeth clashing together.

She wheeled blindly, knocked her hand against the sideboard and saw the empty spaces where the silver candlesticks that had been Mrs Ellis's pride, and the presentation silver cigarette box that had been his, had stood.

As she moved leadenly towards the door, one foot kicked a small object, so light she almost missed the faint rattling noise it made. She picked it up, held it out before her, revolving it clumsily in her fingers. The shuddering ceased abruptly. It seemed for a while that her heart was stifling to death in her breast, that the loathsome, unspeakable scene her brain conceived had frozen her limbs to ice. It was as though some unearthly sixth sense had drawn apart a black curtain and revealed for her eyes alone a fragment of time past. It couldn't be, she screamed silently, not a thing so bestial and vile. Ah, but it could be, the half-stifled voice of reason whispered back. She, and she alone, knew that the fiendish picture that had surfaced in her mind, could have been acted out in this room during the long, secret hours of the night.

Crossing the road, she stumbled at both curbs as though she were drunk. Back in her neat home, she managed at the fourth attempt to poke her finger into a digit on the telephone dial, spin it three times.

TWO

Martin Ellis put the Rover in the car park behind The Three Kings and congratulated himself on his timing: twenty minutes late for his appointment. The thought of Redditch cooling his heels and fanning his temper served to pay off a few old scores. He double-checked the locks on the 3-litre Rover which, as long as no one suspected it was hired, was visible proof that he had no need to count his pounds in hundreds much less in tens, and set out on the five-minute stroll that would bring him to the offices of Brown, Redditch & Brownlow, Solicitors at Law.

He was less interested in categorising the changes in the skyline, that now included giant cooling ovens and high-rise flats, than in confirming from his reflection in shop windows that his person could not be faulted. Martin Ellis was twenty-nine, 5′ 10″ tall. Though his outward mien was confident and openhanded, his personality was complex with a wide range of facets tailored to fit different requirements. His cinnamon-coloured hair that was, rather curiously, an exact match to his eyes, was fashionably long in the neck but not too long and had sufficient wave to make it appear thicker than it was. His face, except for a too indefinite chin, was pleasing enough, but when he was tense or unsure it took on a mean shadow. He checked each garment: well-cut light weight mid-blue jacket, grey slacks, bright-hued shirt and tie, soft-skin boots. The job completed, he awarded his reflection a congratulatory smile.

A placard propped in front of a newstand caught his eye.

ELLIS MURDER. MAN HELPING POLICE. His hand dived to his pocket for coppers, then withdrew. By the time he gave his name to the girl in the front office of Brown, Redditch & Brownlow, the heave of revulsion had subsided. He reminded himself forcibly that this was the day on which he was, literally, to be reborn, the misfortunes, misjudgments and sheer devil's own luck by which he'd been dogged, were to be redeemed. And not before time. It had been a long haul. Too long!

Arnold Redditch, the sole elderly survivor of the original three partners, did not rise from behind his desk to greet his visitor. He had known Martin Ellis since birth and, but for the fact that he was an avowed agnostic, would undoubtedly have been pressured into standing as his godfather. That Martin made no apology for his unpunctuality did not surprise him. What did was his appearance: that of a young man riding along in a comfortable income bracket.

He said formally: "I am sorry we were unable to contact you until after your father's funeral. Had you left a forwarding address with your employer this unhappy delay would not have occurred."

"I had no means of knowing ahead where I'd be. I stayed at a different hotel each night."

Redditch said distantly: "Your father's murder was given good coverage on the radio and in the newspapers."

Martin looked pained. "It was my first break for eighteen months. Except for the headlines I didn't bother much with newspapers, and it wasn't mentioned on any radio bulletin I listened to. I didn't hear about it until I got back to the hotel yesterday morning. I immediately contacted the police, and you."

Redditch glanced at a note on his pad. "Inspector Naylor, who is one of the police officers working on the case, wishes to see you as soon as possible. Perhaps you would look in at the Police Station after you leave here?"

"If it's necessary, okay. But I can't think why it should be. A police officer interviewed me in London yesterday after-

6

noon. Not that I could give him any help. I haven't set foot in Coldbridge for eight years."

Redditch scrupulously made no comment but limited himself to one darting glance of contempt. It was wasted. Martin said with a ring of satisfaction: "According to a newspaper placard outside, the police have a man in custody helping them with their enquiries. I take it that means they've got the murdering thug?"

"During the past week a number of men have been questioned by the police though none of them has been charged with your father's murder."

Martin burst out: "It was brutal, vile . . . inhuman."

"I agree." Redditch had gone to school with Mervyn Ellis, been his friend for half a century, but he had no inclination to comment on their relationship to Mervyn's only child. He untied a file, abstracted a document which he handed to Martin. "A copy of your father's will. You will see that I am named as his sole executor."

As Martin's fingers grasped the fold of paper that was his passport to a new life, paradoxically all faith in his future suddenly caved in, leaving him at the mercy of a spasm of schoolboyish funk. He fought it off. Who else was there for the old man to leave his money to but his only child? He said: "I imagine it's all pretty straightforward?"

"Yes. Except for two legacies your father's estate is willed to you. He left the sum of £1,000 to Mrs Martha Selby in gratitude for her services to him and his late wife, and £1,000 to Miss Elaine Lowther for her unfailing kindness to him during his years of widowhood."

Martin had to send his glance into a dive to hide his blinding shock and outrage. One thousand pounds to a doddering old charwoman who would not live long enough to spend it; and worse, oh, infinitely worse, bitter as gall, a thousand pounds of *his* money to that sly bitch, Elaine Lowther. His half-stupefied reaction was that this was the means by which she'd paid him back.

There was a moment's silence while he fought for control

7

over his voice, then he asked: "What's the value of my father's estate? Approximately?"

"Until the house is sold, the mortgage repaid and your father's overdraft at the bank cleared, it isn't possible to give you even an approximate figure."

The second shock robbed him of all power to dissemble. His mouth gaped. His father, a retired bank manager with an adequate pension, abstemious, even parsimonious, raising a mortgage, running an overdraft! He blurted out: "I don't get it. Why the mortgage, the overdraft?"

"During the last eighteen months of her life your mother was in a private nursing home. She underwent two major operations for abdominal cancer. To pay the surgeon's fees, the nursing home, your father raised a £1,500 mortgage on the house. When this proved insufficient the bank granted him an overdraft of £2,000. Since your mother's death, he'd gradually reduced this to £1,200. Naturally the repayment of the mortgage and the bank overdraft are the first charges on his estate. Next come the legacies; you are the residual legatee."

The man who had been cheated of his inheritance spluttered: "But there is a free National Health Service: hospital, doctors, surgeons, the lot! Free!"

"Your father wished your mother to be privately treated, to have every comfort it was in his power to provide for her."

Money down the drain, his money! He snatched at what remained. "How much is the house worth?"

Redditch was not prepared to express an opinion. He advised Martin to consult Kenneth Robson of Robson & Bates, the estate agents on Market Street.

But Martin needed a figure instantly, one from which had to be deducted the total of the sum he'd already done in his head: £4,700. He insisted: "But you must have some idea of property values in Coldbridge. £6,000? £7,000?"

Redditch repeated it was a matter for an expert. Granted property prices were inflated but many other factors were

8

involved. Hartfield Road was no longer a first-class residential area. A council estate was scheduled to be built on the open land at the rear; a ring-road development scheme was under review. Added to which the house had fallen into a poor state of repair and was lacking in all modern amenities.

He handed Martin a ring containing half a dozen keys, asked for his signature on a formal receipt. The official valuers would be in touch with him to make an appointment to assess the house and its contents for probate. Meanwhile no article must be removed. The warning delivered, he stood to signal the interview was at an end.

Out in the street Martin continued to toss the figures around in his head: a minimum of £1,500, a maximum of, say, £2,500. It wasn't enough, nowhere near. Folk was demanding £15,000 for a half share in the hotel: £7,500 down, the balance to be paid over five years. What's more, the old miser wanted it in cash: that way he'd win himself leeway for a tax fiddle.

Opposite the newsstand where the placard was still in its wire frame, the window lettering of Robson & Bates skimmed across his vision, made him want to gag. When she'd menaced him like a creeping plague, Elaine Lowther had been employed there as a typist, probably still was, the richer by £1,000 of his money! To admit her name to enter his thoughts was like voluntarily putting his head in a pillory. As a temporary solace for the monstrous blows fate had dealt him in the last hour, he strode into The Three Kings. He'd no intention of going near the police until he was well fortified by drink and food—in that order.

Elaine put a batch of contracts before Kenneth Robson, aware but unmoved by his barely contained chagrin. On Saturday afternoon Robson & Bates operated on a shift system, the telephone and counter manned by two juniors with a senior member of the staff on hand, whom this particular Saturday afternoon should have been Elaine. On

Friday afternoon, having learned from a telephone call to Mr Redditch, that Martin would be calling on him at noon on Saturday, Elaine had asked Kenneth if it would be okay if she switched her Saturday duty to the following week. Kenneth was agreeable so long as Graham Cheetham was willing to substitute. Graham was.

But Graham Cheetham's wife had gone into premature labour in the early hours of Saturday morning. Her husband was pacing the corridor outside the hospital delivery room, and it wasn't reasonable to suppose that Robson & Bates would set eyes on him until Monday morning.

So, with the senior partner, Harold Bates, salmon fishing in Scotland, old reliable was expected to cancel whatever date she'd made for Saturday afternoon, remain on duty. All morning Kenneth had been silently pressuring her to make the offer. When she failed him, he was shattered. In an emergency Elaine, not only a privileged employee, but a family friend, was depriving him of his Saturday afternoon's golf, leaving him to man the office, his sole support a dim-witted typist and a singularly inept trainee who, last week, had been charged with dangerous driving and only retained his licence by the skin of his teeth.

As he watched Elaine's neat rear disappear into her own office, he reflected sourly that, when it came to the crunch, you couldn't trust any woman, not even one whom he would have sworn would have put the firm's interests ahead of her own.

Although Elaine could have offered to do the afternoon shift, postponed her meeting with Martin until evening or even Sunday morning, her conscience was untroubled. There was only a remote chance that he would be come and gone from 8, Hartfield Road in the space of the afternoon, but she wasn't taking that chance.

She lifted the jacket of a new suit off its hanger. It was featherweight navy cashmere, with a snow-white silk under-blouse. When she'd retied the bow she took a long minute to examine herself in the three-quarter length mirror, to assess the transformation that eight years had wrought in Elaine Lowther. Slimmer, more co-ordinated, with a skin of assurance that did a fair job of hiding the areas of chaos within. At heart was she any different? That was a question she couldn't answer yet.

As she walked to the parking yard reserved for Robson & Bates's employees, she stopped abruptly, marked the landscape around her. When next she stood sandwiched between the rearing side of Woolworth's and Olson's garage, she'd have seen Martin, and the pattern of her inner world might be drastically redesigned. Or it might not.

Martin, drinking coffee in the dining room of The Three Kings, refused the waiter's offer of brandy. Alongside the major accounting was a niggardly juggling with pounds and pence: his bill for three whiskies before lunch, a bottle of Hock with his filet steak and Camembert. After the morning's calamitous news he could not afford to squander any of his meagre savings. Yet the compulsion to treat himself handsomely had been the only compensation at hand for the barefaced robbery to which he had been subjected. What his half-senile old father would have termed, showing the flag.

At Saturday lunchtime the dining room was crowded. He was too absorbed in his mental arithmetic to scan the faces for any that were familiar, but he was vaguely aware that one of a couple of women lunching three tables away had allowed her glance to hang on him. If she'd been the type, he'd have suspected the opening gambit in a pickup, but she wasn't. Or he didn't judge so.

When she paid the bill, she murmured a few words to her companion and walked over to his table. His first impression was that her triangular face under the simple but rakish green hat evinced suppressed merriment, like that of a mischievous child about to pull off a joke. "You don't remember me, do you, Martin?"

"Give me a moment . . ." He was on his feet, his smile

designed to charm, offering her his hand, conscious in that first instant of the faint drift of French perfume, the expensive tan lizard handbag she rested on the table.

Her laugh was a low, husky sound of outright amusement. "Okay, own up, you haven't a clue. All right, I'll let you off the hook. Sheila Clark, now Sheila Bostock."

"Sheila! Of course." He pulled out the facing chair. "In another second I'd have got it. It was the hat that foxed me. If I'd seen your hair, I'd have recognised you instantly. Sheila! This is terrific. Sit down . . . please."

"Only for a moment."

The Sheila Clark he'd known briefly when she'd sworn she was seventeen but was probably sixteen, had been a skinny, graceless, giggling girl in whom he'd lost interest when, on their third date, the grandfather with whom she lived—rumour had it she was illegitimate—had lain in wait for him at the front door of his near-slum house, knocked the living daylights out of him with a yard broom. He beckoned the waiter. "More coffee, please."

"Not for me." A residue of amusement lingered in her voice. "The friend I lunched with is waiting for me in the foyer. But I just had to say hello." Her voice and face sobered to express commiseration. "For one thing I wanted to say how ghastly it was about your father. I can't say how sorry . . ." She blinked, embarrassed and at a loss.

"Thank you." Momentarily he bowed his head. "I still can't believe it. Murdering a helpless old man for a couple of silver candlesticks and a cigarette box! Even in this age of violence you just can't take it in . . . not when it's your own father."

They exchanged a discreet querying glance, testing one another as to whether the subject could be decently closed. She chanced it. "How long have you been back in Coldbridge?"

"A matter of hours." He glanced at the rings on her left hand. "You're married! Well, naturally! To anyone I know?"

12

"I don't think so. Desmond only moved here after you left. He teaches at Bychurch Comprehensive School."

And did his wife extraordinarily well on a schoolteacher's salary. Martin possessed a highly developed talent for assessing the precise cash value of any article, and Sheila's clothes and accessories were more geared to the income of a stockbroker than a schoolteacher. "How long have you been married?"

"Five years next month." She rose. "Martin, I really do have to go. Anne loathes hanging around. How long are you staying?"

"Long enough, I hope, to see the police get their hands on the thug who murdered Dad. But I can't hang on too long as I'm in the middle of a business deal: in the process of buying a half-share in an hotel of which I'm currently the manager."

"Sounds an exciting proposition. Where is the hotel?"

"In Bayswater. The Eglantine. At the moment too high a proportion of the guests are aged widows eking out their lives on sherry and chitchat. But it has potential and I'm setting my sights on the tourist trade."

"To buy even half an hotel in Bayswater must need a fortune!"

Not for a sleazy run-down dump like the Eglantine—but she wasn't to know that. "A fair sum. But the property is leasehold with only another ten years of the lease to run. There may well be development when it falls in, so it's a do or die operation. Make good in ten years and be ready to move on and up . . . or else!" he grinned boyishly. "A challenge. Suits me."

Watching her closely, he saw that he'd captured her interest. Her skin was a redhead's skin, creamy magnolia, unmarred by a single freckle. If her eyes had been blue or green instead of midbrown, she'd have been model material. Even so, she wasn't far off. By what extraordinary process had Sheila Clark, scrawny, raucous-voiced, in a matter of ten years or so, been transformed into this delectable, expensively turned out young woman? Surely she couldn't have accomplished the metamorphosis alone! So who was her Pygmalion?

She picked up her handbag. "Well, it's certainly been fun seeing you after all this time. And good luck with the hotel deal."

The prospect of contact between them severed was surprisingly painful. Five minutes before he hadn't been able to recall her name; now he was intrigued, his senses brushed with excitement. He openly begged: "Couldn't we have a drink some time, with your husband? I'd like to meet him. Here, say, or anywhere you suggest."

She looked doubtful, but as though she were relishing the moment of deliberation, the suspense in which she kept him. Then she threw him a veiled but sharply appraising glance that told him that the examination had been a reciprocal process: her amazement in him as genuine as his in her. Maybe, too, the tingling of emotions wasn't only on his side.

"On Sunday evenings we usually have a buffet supper. Friends drop in any time between seven and eight. If you're free, why don't you come along?"

"Thanks. I'd love to. Where do I find you?"

"5, Willow Close. Take the North road out of town and after about a mile you'll see it on your left. You've got a car?"

He nodded, smiling forgiveness at the question.

"Fine, I'll expect you." Her smile turned frankly sensual, her eyes bright with amusement or mischief. It was impossible to tell which.

He watched her legs that tapered to deliciously slender ankles until they disappeared from view and marvelled that, during the doldrums of his life, when round every corner, like a personal nemesis, Elaine Lowther lay in wait, this fledgling beauty had been developing. That smell of money, and surely big money? The only answer that suggested itself was that she'd married a schoolteacher with a handsome private income. The grandfather—the grandmother had died a year or two before he'd become aware of Sheila's existence—who'd lived in a dreary terrace house at the back of the railway sidings, hadn't had a bean.

Detective Inspector Naylor had the face of a tired bloodhound, the sagging torso of a sedentary man. He looked older than his forty years and this morning, after a gruelling six wholly profitless days on the Ellis murder, he had every reason to. His superior officer, Detective Chief Superintendent Frank Drummond, himself pressured from above, was getting thinner tempered, edgier by the hour. Every breaker-and-enterer, robbery-with-violence merchant and petty thief within a radius of twenty-five miles of Coldbridge had been pulled in and, like Tug Richie, two months out of Strangeways for knocking an old woman senseless and stealing her purse, released on account of an iron-cast alibi, or insufficient evidence.

Wearing the expression of a man who has suffered every possible variation of the species *homo sapiens*, and with only four hours' sleep the previous night, he had no impulse to rise to his feet at the sight of Martin Ellis. Instead he waved towards a facing chair that Sergeant Tanner had placed ready before he left for a belated canteen lunch.

"Good of you to look in, Mr Ellis," he said perfunctorily.

"Only too anxious to help in any way I can." Food, drink, plus the revivifying effect of the meeting with Sheila, had relaxed Martin to the extent that he was prepared to suffer a purposeless interview with a semblance of grace. "But I was a bit mystified at the message you left with Redditch asking to see me. A police officer called on me in London yesterday and asked me a whole string of questions, so I can't imagine what further information I can give you. It's eight years since I left Coldbridge and, having been abroad most of the time, there's been no opportunity for me to visit my father." He lowered his voice a tone, formed his lips into a grieving line. "Now, as you can imagine, this is a source of bitter regret to me."

Naylor reached for a file, opened it and glanced down the top sheet. "Most of the time you were in South Africa, Johannesburg to be exact, but you also visited Australia and Canada. You had a job in Johannesburg?"

"Yes. With a top-class catering firm."

"You also served as a steward on cruise liners. It was on one of these, returning from Australia, that you met your present employer, Mr Sebastian Folk?"

"That's so. The manager of the hotel he owns was on the point of retiring. He offered me the job and I accepted."

"A job you still hold. During your eighteen months in London you felt no urge to visit your father who was widowed and in poor health?"

"Plenty of urge." Martin countered the reproach with spirit. "What I lacked was opportunity."

Naylor turned a page. "Last Sunday morning, the day after your father was murdered, you left for a holiday in the West Country."

"Since I hadn't had more than the odd day off in my eighteen months at the Eglantine, I was bushed, desperately in need of a break. I had fixed another week's leave for the end of this month. That I intended spending with my father."

"You arrived back at the Hotel Eglantine at 11:30 yesterday morning. Who broke the news of your father's murder to you?"

"Mr Folk. When I'd recovered from the initial shock that practically knocked me out, I got in touch with the nearest police station and also with my father's solicitor Mr Redditch. As I mentioned a police sergeant came to see me. I believe his name was Blackboys. He told me that my father had been buried that morning."

There was a heavy silence during which Naylor brooded over the third sheet in the folder. Martin broke it. "I saw a newspaper placard saying you were holding someone for questioning. Does that mean you've caught the brute who murdered my father?"

"I'm afraid not. He was released half an hour ago. Now, Mr Ellis, I wonder if you'd mind going over your movements for the 9th and 10th of September. That is last Saturday and Sunday."

Martin protested: "What possible bearing can they have on my father's horrible death?"

"Mr Ellis, it is my duty to check that Sergeant Blackboys recorded your statement correctly. It's an incorrigible habit of ours the public find tedious and irksome. Double-checking, then treble-checking."

Martin sighed with resignation. "It seems a waste of your time and mine, but if you insist, okay. Some months ago, when his doctor told him that his health might benefit from cleaner air, Mr Folk bought a village pub in Outhwell, Leicestershire. Perhaps I should explain that ten years ago he had polio, since when he has been confined to a wheelchair. Extensive alterations are being made to the downstairs living quarters in the pub, corridors and doors widened, ramps to replace steps and so on. As he is hoping to retire there at Christmas, he intended to check on the progress of the alterations, but at the last minute he didn't feel up to making the journey and asked me to go for him. I agreed, though actually I was due to start my holiday that Saturday morning.

"I left London around ten, got to Outhwell for a late lunch, which I had with the publican and his wife who are there until Christmas. We were joined by the architect and builder. I left about five, or it might have been a little later. On the spur of the moment I decided to make a detour on the way back to the village of Duchberry in Bedfordshire. A school friend of mine had moved there; I'd spent a couple of holidays with him and thought I'd look him up. But I missed my way, and when I eventually reached the village, I found the family had moved away so long ago that no one even remembered their name.

17

"At a guess I'd say I was back on the M.1. around eleven. I stopped at the first service station I came to, had a meal and pushed on. I reached the hotel somewhere between one and two, let myself in and went to bed. Next morning I reported on the progress of the alterations to Mr Folk and was on my way west some time around noon. I spent Sunday night at Shaftesbury and the other five at different hotels that I named in my statement to Sergeant Blackboys."

Naylor looked up at him. His dun-coloured heavy-lidded eyes were brighter and sharper than when Martin entered the room. "What car do you drive, Mr Ellis?"

"A car goes with the job, a Ford Cortina. I used that for the drive to and from Outhwell. In case Mr Folk needed the Cortina while I was away, I hired a car, a Rover 3 litre, for the trip to the West Country, and to drive up here."

"What colour are the cars?"

"The Rover, gunmetal. The Cortina cream. Inspector, I'd like to know why you're interested in the colour of both cars."

There was no answer that Naylor was prepared to give or, in fact, could give at this stage. On a fine night the laybys on the main road bordering Fenny's Slope behind Hartfield Road were a popular parking place for necking couples, but the night Mervyn Ellis had been murdered had been the reverse of fine, and they'd only received reports of three vehicles seen in the vicinity. A Morris 1100, either grey or blue, a white or cream car, make unspecified, both empty, and a cream Cortina, with a girl and a youth in the front seat; the letters of the number plate of which had fortunately lodged in the memory of a reliable witness.

The Cortina was owned by Mrs Knight, a widow who lived in Crossfield Road. She had played bridge with neighbours from 8 P.M. until 10:30 P.M. on the night of Saturday the 9th. When she left home her car was standing in the drive. When she returned it had vanished. She'd telephoned the police to report the theft and had then been forced to telephone them a second time at 7 A.M. next morning to announce that it had been returned during the night.

Not a single fingerprint had been found on the car—not even one of Mrs Knight's. The Forensic boys had vacuumed the upholstery and floor clean of hair, fluff, fibre, grit, and dirt before the car had been returned to Mrs Knight. Meanwhile Naylor was no nearer knowing whether it had been "borrowed" by a youth to take his girl for a ride or for a more sinister purpose that linked up with the Ellis murder.

"What may seem irrelevant to you, may not be so to us. I'm afraid you'll have to bear with us, Mr Ellis." Naylor closed the folder, stood up, and gave his droopy smile. "Well, thanks for your co-operation. How long are you staying in Coldbridge?"

"No longer than I can help. I'm needed in London."

"What's going to happen to the hotel when Mr Folk retires to his country pub at Christmas?"

Martin paused momentarily before answering, then decided he was under no obligation to volunteer information to the police on the personal deal pending between himself and Folk. "That's still a matter for negotiation. Goodbye, Inspector."

"You'll be staying at 8, Hartfield Road until you return to London?"

"Yes, of course."

"I'd be obliged if you would let me know before you leave and naturally, if there is any development, I'll get in touch with you. Oh, and there's just one other small matter. We'd like your fingerprints. Purely for elimination purposes, of course. There are still a few sets of prints in the house that we haven't accounted for."

"Fingerprints! You must be joking, Inspector. I haven't been inside the house for eight years. Fingerprints after eight years!"

"Even so, I assure you, Mr Ellis, that it is not unlikely that somewhere in that house there is a set of your fingerprints. And if so, as I have explained, we need them for elimination purposes." He indicated the figure, summoned by a push button, who stood in the doorway. "Sergeant Tanner will see to it. It won't take more than five minutes."

For a while after he was alone Naylor gazed at the space that Martin Ellis had occupied, as if his physical presence was still visible. An unloving—maybe even a callous—son, with a glib tongue, so much was blatantly obvious, but beyond that condemnation he was not prepared at the moment further to define his judgment.

THREE

At two o'clock Elaine positioned herself at a point in her bedroom that afforded her an unimpeded view of the Ellis house while shielding her from sight. Nothing in her behaviour struck her as departing from the norm. Like all fanatics she was blessedly unconscious of her fanaticism.

Only a couple of cars passed. It was a dead hour with families, home from Saturday morning shopping, eating lunch or already sprawled before their television sets watching the sports programme. No more than a couple of cars passed. Waiting, the eyes of her mind re-created the frenzied scene of six days ago when police cars, sirens screaming, had spurted into Hartfield Road, taken root there, together with a mobile canteen, for all Sunday and most of Monday. Tracker dogs and men with Geiger counters had combed every inch of Fenny's Slope and the gardens lining the road. Each house had been visited by an interrogation squad, and Elaine had spent two hours at Police Headquarters.

At a quarter to three the gunmetal Rover closed in at the opposite curb. Stillness held Elaine so rigid she scarcely seemed to breathe. After a first lightning scan she advanced, then retreated behind the shield of a curtain, absorbed in recording the quality of Martin's clothes, his noticeably inflated confidence. The solidly expensive but not flashy car rendered meaningless Mrs Ellis's constant terror that her darling boy wasn't getting enough to eat, and Mr Ellis's foreboding that his only son was incapable of supporting himself. Yet, prospering, how could Martin, being Martin, have resisted the temptation to flaunt his prosperity before his parents? Granted the car could be borrowed or hired, and one set of smart clothes bought for a comparatively modest sum—the purpose to impress. But to impress whom? There was no one left to impress but herself.

After trial and error he found the garage key, opened the door and promptly slammed it shut. As she could have told him, and surely he should have remembered, it was too crammed with junk to accommodate a car. He unlocked the front door, closed it behind him and was blotted from sight. She decided to give him three-quarters of an hour. Even so, she dragged a chair forward, kept her eyes on the house, watching the windows for shadows of movement. None was visible. Except for the Rover at the curb it might have been as empty of life as it had been last Sunday morning when she'd received no answer to her: "Hello, Mr Ellis."

At ten past three, having smoothed her hair, she went downstairs. Her face as cool and composed as a young nun's, she opened the front door and, turning to close it, was shaken by a feeling of revulsion towards her home. Her father had died of a coronary five years ago, so why, no longer subject to his will that held sacred the curtains, furniture, and cooking pans her mother's hands had touched, hadn't she sold the lot, bought and furnished a modern house or an open-plan flat? The term prisoner spelled itself in her head. Was that what she was, a prisoner of her own emotions? If so, her sentence might be coming to an end. Contrarily, it might endure for ever.

As the latch clicked, she experienced one of those flashes of insight that occasionally ripped her apart, exposing Elaine Lowther to Elaine Lowther. A woman morbidly, neurotically obsessed with the past? Or a woman with a long memory, hell-bent on revenge? It was, she answered herself, simpler than that: she was determined to prove or disprove that terrorising backtrack into time that had chilled her heart to ice six days ago.

Once inside the door, Martin started on a lightning survey of the house and contents, working from the attic downwards. Most of the furniture was prewar multiple store variety, though there were one or two genuine antiques his mother had inherited from her family. She'd been a chronic hoarder of knickknacks and there was a cabinet in the sitting room loaded with an assortment of china. Most of it was rubbish, but there was a basket encrusted with flowers that could be Meissen, and what looked like two pieces of Dresden.

He stood back and surveyed his father's bureau, solid mahogany inlaid with brass. At today's values it might, with luck, fetch a couple of hundred. A paltry twenty ten-pound notes for Folk to grab with his brown-mottled hands! He'd first laid eyes on his employer when, serving as a cabin steward, he'd found Sebastian Folk made a prisoner in his bed by the chronic seasickness of his manservant, Beckley. First-class, outside cabin, gold tops to the crystal bottles in his toilet case, and a fat wallet on the bedside table. Martin, sniffing wealth, had played his cards with skill and patience, humouring and pampering a crippled, mean-tempered old man who had money to squander on himself. By the time the ship docked at Southampton he was on Folk's payroll. After eighteen months of hard labour his ambition was within snatching distance: a half-share in a run-down third-class hotel, a leaping-off point to being his own boss. Except that he wasn't within sight of securing the down payment. There being no profit in subjecting himself to a further agonising session of adding and subtracting, he turned to the bureau. The top contained no more than a thin bundle of his own letters and postcards, a clip of receipted bills, rubber bands, balled-up lengths of string, a couple of old-fashioned fountain pens and upwards of twenty sticks of sealing wax.

The first drawer was crammed with household account books dating back to the year his parents had married—when his father had been forty-five and his mother in her late thirties—and rolls of his school reports. The second drawer contained his father's stamp albums. He awarded them as a perk to himself on the off-chance that some of the stamps were as rare and valuable as his father had claimed. No need for the official valuer to know of their existence.

The bottom drawer appeared to be stuffed solid with old newspapers and periodicals, but right at the back was a weighty object wrapped in coarse canvas. When he unfolded it he found himself staring at a revolver and a box of ammunition. That his father, an avowed pacifist, a law-abiding citizen *par excellence,* should possess a Webley & Scott .38 double action revolver, astounded him.

Checking it wasn't loaded, he folded the canvas into a square, laid it on the rickety gate-legged table, placed the revolver and the box of silver-nosed bullets on top of it beside the stamp albums. On impulse he lifted the flower-encrusted basket that might or might not be Meissen from the cabinet. Modest pickings, but all he dare lift. Redditch had been in the habit of playing chess with his father one evening a week and could be guaranteed to have made a mental inventory of the contents of the house.

When the doorbell rang, his first reaction was to ignore it. It could hardly be Sheila and there was no one else in Coldbridge whom he wished to see—certainly not one of his father's senile old cronies who, due to his parents' late marriage, were nearer two generations removed from him than one.

In the end, because the caller went on ringing the bell, he answered it, and immediately cursed himself. Any normal girl in Elaine Lowther's shoes would have cut him dead in the street instead of having the gall to stand smiling on the doorstep.

"Hello, Martin. When I saw the car outside I guessed you were back. How are you?"

"Up to my ears sorting through Dad's papers, pressed for time."

She put a hand on the door, but he resisted the pressure.

Seeming unaware of the rebuff, she remarked: "I left you a few packets of food, and some milk, eggs and cheese in the fridge. Enough to cover your breakfast and a snack if you need one."

"Thanks," he said so grudgingly that it should have put her to flight.

Unmoved by the arm that barred her entrance, she asked: "May I come in for a minute?"

"Some other time, Elaine."

"No, now," she insisted in that cool, adamant voice that sent a cold draught down his spine. It was a replica of his mother's, a woman who'd worn a mask compounded of faint abstraction, gentle-temper and good-nature, under which she'd masked a will of iron and an assumption of some divine right to have her lightest wish fulfilled—as it invariably was. "We must talk about the money your father left me. You didn't imagine I'd accept it, did you?"

In the second that the words winded him, she pushed against the door and, before he could stop her, had walked as though she owned the house along the hall and into the sitting room. Her glance instantly marked the open drawers of the bureau, the objects on the table. Her eyes widened fractionally. "A gun! Is it yours?"

"No, father's. I found it tucked away at the back of a drawer."

She scanned the face she'd learned as a child to read for evidence of distortion of the truth and finding none, slowly shook her head. "I simply can't imagine your father keeping a gun. It must be a relic left over from the war that he'd forgotten. What will you do with it? Hand it over to the police?"

"Probably."

Caught off-guard by a rush of nostalgia she ran an affectionate hand over the stamp albums. "He hadn't opened them for years. Even with his new glasses he couldn't see well enough. Oh, and the Meissen basket. When I was a child your mother used to let me hold it. One day I accidentally knocked it against the table; that's why one of the rosebuds is chipped."

He hadn't noticed the chip but found it typical that she should rob him of two thirds of the basket's worth by reducing it to damaged goods. But the electrifying words she'd spoken on the doorstep spurred him to a gesture that might pay a dividend. "Why don't you take it as a keepsake of her?"

"Don't all the contents of the house have to be kept intact for probate?"

She'd always been a bit of a barrack-room lawyer and eight years had not ridden her of the trait. He answered, riled: "You're surely not questioning my right to examine my parents' personal effects! And as it's a job that will take some time and I've not much to waste . . ."

She gave him a glance that while it contained no direct reproach, dried the words on his tongue. Between the waxy lids it held the adamancy he dreaded. He thought, as he'd thought a thousand times, she might have been his mother's daughter. Invincible.

Yet her voice was uncontentious. "I should have thought you'd have wished to have the money side settled. Your father left me a thousand pounds as a mark of appreciation for what I was able to do for your mother while she was alive and, later, for him when he was alone and housebound." Her glance, withdrawn into grief, momentarily held his, then she shook her head in disclaimer. "Trifles, that took no time at all, that I loved doing. I don't want to be paid for them with money that I'm sure you regard as yours."

He ignored the typical sly dig. "But you haven't a choice, have you? Legally that money can't be handed over to anyone but you? Redditch drew up the will, he's the executor, so you may be sure there are no loopholes. You'll get that thousand pounds whether you want it or not."

She gave him a long, calculating glance, noting his moods were as mercurial as ever: heady elation one moment, deadening despair the next. She knew them as intimately as her own. "A simple transaction sets it right. When I've banked the cheque from Redditch, I can make out another to you for the same amount."

He needed time to get his breath. To gain that time he bent to close the bottom drawer of the bureau. Spurred on by his mother, Elaine had shamelessly and relentlessly pursued—no devoured—him since her teens. When she had eventually triumphed, in an act of desperation and sheer terror of them both, he'd sprung the trap by bolting. It followed she must bear him a grudge. Granted her parents had been comfortably off on her father's earnings as Borough Treasurer, plus money which her mother had inherited from the sale of the family drapery business, which meant Elaine must now be well endowed. Even so, voluntarily to kiss goodbye to a tax-free gift of a thousand pounds was crazy unless you were certain of a return. He swallowed a great lump that was half choking him. After all this time, was she still after him?

He swung round on his haunches, challenged: "Why the hell should you make me a present of a thousand pounds?"

As though deliberating to herself, she paused before answering. "Since I don't wish to be paid for small kindnesses I did for your father out of love, you've a moral right to it. Maybe, too, you need it more than I do."

He looked up, that mingling of hate and fear she'd always evoked in him, a red mist before his eyes. He managed to jeer: "The prodigal returns without a bean; thankful for a hand-out!"

She examined him with cool, unshadowed grey eyes as he stumbled clumsily to his feet. "Obviously not, but that doesn't mean you couldn't put a thousand pounds to good use." She held her voice under control, but the strain was audible. "If your father had died naturally perhaps I wouldn't have reacted so strongly against taking the money. But he died in terror, appalling agony, screaming for help . . . and no one heard." She paused, drew in her breath sharply. "I found him, and I'll never forget it, never." She repeated in a taut appalled voice: "Never."

He turned his back on her, snapped: "Don't you think I care! What do you imagine the way Dad died does to me?"

"I don't know, do I!"

Though he could not see her, he felt, as though it was a physical touch, her eyes glued hard to his spine. Back in her old role: the watcher in his own home, from across the street, even when she'd been a puny, motherless child whom his mother had taken to heart and henceforth groomed as her future daughter-in-law. And no matter what tactics he'd employed to discourage her, she'd stayed obstinately un-discouraged, certain she'd nail him in the end. At all costs, the chill invading his bones, contagion from a mind he be-lieved to be sick, had to be beaten off. "I wouldn't have thought you owed me any favours."

"Oh, you're right," she said lightly. "I don't. This isn't a favour. It's a simple business transaction."

Not simple, he raged. Nothing was simple. It was one thing to show Folk a copy of his father's will in which he bequeathed his property and possessions to his only son, and another explaining he wasn't the sole legatee, about the mortgage and the overdraft. Oh, Christ, the mess and complications, when everything should have been clean-cut!

Her tone suddenly changed to one of interested enquiry. "Your father said a few months ago that you were working in an hotel."

"I manage an hotel," he corrected, "one in which I'm in the process of buying a half-share."

Again she marvelled at the contradiction: of Martin mak-ing good and not flaunting his success. She admitted certain changes eight years had wrought in him, but was convinced they were no more than surface scratches. Basically, she was sure his reactions, intentions, even the direction of his thoughts, were as plain to her as they'd been eight years ago. And always, horrific, in a never-sleeping corner of her mind, was that tiny parcel wrapped in tissue, hidden in the

28

bottom of her jewel box. She enquired: "Have you been into the old dining room, where your father slept?"

"No," he snapped, resenting the question. "What good would it do him my getting harrowed and shaken up?"

"It's been scrubbed and cleaned, the bed burnt. There was nothing else to do with it when the police had finished. Mr Redditch collected the remainder of your mother's silver: the candelabras, the big epergne she was so proud of. I thought you'd like to know they were safe in the bank."

He nodded perfunctory thanks. Solid silver, late Regency. He tried to estimate how much they would fetch. Probably several hundred, and gnawed at the sore that it would be months before he knew. His eye traced the faded curtains sagging from their hooks, the threadbare carpet: probably not more than a thousand for the contents of the entire house including silver and the bureau. Between two and three thousand towards the £7,500 he'd promised Folk would be in the bank before the deed was drawn up.

She lifted the flower basket and set it back in its place in the cabinet. "I was thinking, with so much to do, why don't you come and have Sunday lunch over the road? You wouldn't have to take time either making yourself a snack or driving into town; anyway, most places are closed on Sunday." She caught the look of sick distaste, and knew it so well her smile turned ironic, and she added: "A couple of other friends of mine are coming to lunch, so that would make four of us. You can stay on after they've left and tell me what you've decided about the money. If you don't wish to accept it, I shall divide it between Help for the Aged and Oxfam."

Suddenly—it was the smile that did it—he was convinced beyond doubt that she was laying a trap for him. She had no intention of making him a present of a thousand pounds: it was bait for some fiendish ploy she was cooking up.

"Thanks," he snapped, "but I've too much to do here to take a couple of hours off."

"But you have to eat," she countered with smooth reason.

"It doesn't involve you in a journey, not even in smartening yourself up. All you have to do is to wash the dust off your hands and cross the road. I'll expect you for a drink at half-past twelve."

She walked with a firm step out of the room, through the hall and out of the house, taking his acceptance for granted. That was what scared him, as though, whatever distance he set between them, somewhere along the line, when he turned a corner, she'd be waiting for him, a destroyer to lay waste his life. The morbidity of the thought shook him. For God's sake, he was acting like the scared, henpecked kid he'd once been. And what was she? A frustrated—more than likely half-cracked—spinster who'd not managed to catch a husband! That sour image of her, plus the fact that she no longer had a fingerhold of power over him, restored his shaken confidence.

FOUR

Shoulders hunched, Robert Downes set off to collect the eight Sunday newspapers out of which he'd rip the heart in under an hour. He was a lithe-bodied, black-haired, blue-eyed young man just past his thirty-second birthday, with a tough but sensitive face, whose most arresting quality was not his physical appearance, but a quickness of mind that was revealed in the lively thrust of his glance.

The Sunday papers had long been the subject of contention between him and his landlady—heated on his part, coolly obdurate on hers.

"But reading the Sundays is part of my job, Miss Letchworth. Damn it, you needn't set eyes on them. I'll be waiting on the doorstep to snatch them out of the arms of the delivery boy. On the pavement, if you like."

"I cannot countenance it, Mr Downes. Sunday is the Lord's Day. My father refused to allow a secular newspaper in the house on Sunday, and I am proud to follow his example. And please be so good as not to swear in my hearing."

This particular morning when he was minus a car—Sunday being the only day he could survive without it and hand it over to the garage for long-overdue servicing—he morosely contemplated changing his digs. But Miss Letchworth was a superb cook, took his irregular appearances with blessed equanimity and having, by surveillance, proved to her satisfaction that he did not bring women of ill-fame into the home of her late sainted father, barring her Lord's Day aberration, was as good as he was likely to find in Coldbridge.

Added to which, since his future was a question mark, was it worth moving? The choice dangled before him: to bed down on the *Evening Argus* where he was sure of the News Desk before the end of the year, or take up the offer from his old Fleet Street paper now under a new editorship. He had to balance an assured if undramatic future against the blood, sweat, and in-fighting of Fleet Street, where the stakes were high but the going rough and tough. That Miss Letchworth's Plymouth Brethren conscience should tip the scales in either direction was so ludicrous that he grinned. A teenager on a bike swerved, gave him so leery a glance that he laughed aloud. She threw her head back, laughed with him, rode on. Her eyes and the colour of her sheet of swinging hair were the same as Elaine's. Maybe at fifteen, sixteen, that was how Elaine had looked. He wondered if she had been born one pace removed from other mortals or if life had forced her into permanent retreat.

The papers a satisfyingly fat roll under his arm, he looked in at the garage to check that Ernie hadn't overslept. He was, thank God, invisible under the car, but growling fiercely. "It's no good you pestering me, Mr Downes. Twelve o'clock I said, and that's when she'll be ready. Not half-past ten."

"Just making sure, Ernie. I've a lunch date and don't fancy walking two miles."

Crossing the common, twenty yards ahead of him, he glimpsed the tall figure of Detective Chief Superintendent Drummond. He whistled. Drummond halted with visible reluctance. Unless there was a major development in the Ellis case, on the score that it was his twenty-fifth wedding anniversary, he was having the day off. Nine guests had been invited to a gala lunch, making twelve round the table. So, though he believed in maintaining good relations with the Press, he was in no mood to be quizzed by Downes. He squared the shoulders of his six-foot frame, set his handsomely designed set of features in an expression of polite acceptance of the hailing, and gave a nod of greeting that was totally lacking in warmth. Drummond was a career policeman, tenaciously ambitious, who had, in his twenties, married a pretty, modestly rich girl, which had done him no harm at all.

"Well, how's it going?" Downes asked briskly.

"How's what going?"

"The Ellis murder hunt. As if you didn't know! When we went to press yesterday you were holding Tug Richie. Still got him?"

"He was released. Alibi proved beyond doubt."

"So no farther forward!"

While gazing straight ahead Drummond addressed him formally. "Mr Downes, I gave three Press conferences last week. Detective Inspector Naylor conducted two. The Press has been kept fully informed of all developments. Are you registering a complaint?"

"Certainly not; merely asking, politely, to be kept in the picture." When Drummond made no reply, he recapitulated helpfully: "The couple of kids seen in the Cortina parked on Fenny's Slope on the Saturday night haven't come forward?"

"No."

"Nor the man who nearly collided with Rosie Chard's car?"

"No."

"And no joy in tracking down the cigarette box and candlesticks?"

"Correct, Mr Downes."

"So we're still stamping on square one!"

About to deliver a crisp answer, there revived in Drummond's mind a conversation he'd had with Naylor the previous afternoon. In a slightly less formal tone, he remarked: "Except that the son, Martin Ellis, arrived in Coldbridge yesterday." He permitted himself a sideways glance at his inquisitor, remembered another, maybe relevant, angle. "If I'm not mistaken you know his old girl friend, Elaine Lowther."

33

"Girl friend! You mean because she lives opposite and they probably trotted off to school together."

"There's more to it than that. When Martin Ellis skipped off taking fifty pounds from the petty cash of the company by which he was employed, he and Elaine Lowther were formally engaged to be married. You mean you didn't know?"

"There's no reason why I should. It happened nearly ten years ago, didn't it?"

"Eight years and three months." They'd come to a parting of the ways. Drummond added: "I'd be interested to know how she reacts to his return."

Downes admitted he'd no right to be shocked, but the shock, darkened by a tinge of despair, was there. "Are you asking me to pry into an episode of her life she'll naturally wish to forget?"

"Not pry, my dear boy. Merely observe."

"Oh, go to hell!"

"I probably shall, in good company." His humour restored, Drummond, with a patronising lift of his hand continued on his way.

Rosie Chard arrived first. She was short, only escaped being plump by drastic though spasmodic dieting, had feather-cut honey hair, round, innocent blue eyes, and with a dimple in each cheek most of the time she looked like a happy cherub. Male patients in her ward were forever making grabs at her which, with an adroitness she'd learnt at thirteen, she effortlessly avoided, leaving no hard feelings on either side. She wore a modest diamond on her left hand that was an outward symbol of the shimmering state of happiness in which she existed. Come December she was to be married to Bruce Gardner, a sergeant in the private army of the Sheik of one of the Trucial States on the Persian Gulf, live by a perpetually blue sea under palm trees and have four children by the man she'd lusted after for three years before he'd given a sign of noticing her existence.

The permanent state of mild euphoria tended to make

her breathless. "I know I'm too early and I'm being a damned nuisance, but with Mum and Dad away the house seems like a morgue. And I wanted to show you the final design for The Gown."

"Final!" Elaine raised an eyebrow. She'd vetted no less than six.

"Final. It's got to be. Madame is getting snooty. I've a nasty idea she'll throw the order back in my face if I don't make up my mind pretty soon. Elaine, love, couldn't you change your mind about being a bridesmaid?"

"Three angelic tots and Bruce's teenage sister; they'll make a perfect retinue."

Rosie scowled. "I know what it is, you've got a hangup about age. What's thirty! Bruce is nine months younger than me, but you don't catch me worrying."

She laid the design on the kitchen table, weighted the corners down with cutlery. "There!" She pondered anxiously. "You don't think that high waist will make me look all bosomy?"

Elaine obediently gave the sketch her serious attention, then smiled into Rosie's face, contorted by the momentous decision she was called upon to make. "No. It tops all the others. If I were you, I'd settle for it. Truly."

The design remained on view for another ten minutes while Rosie surveyed it from every angle. "I suppose you're right," she conceded. "It's just that I can't bear not to look perfect for Bruce. Okay. Done." She gave a little shiver. "Want me to lay the table for you?"

"If you would. The drinks are out."

"Four?" Rosie queried, popping her head through the hatch in the dining room. "You, me, and Robert, and who else?"

"Martin. Martin Ellis." She braced herself for Rosie's reaction.

It was bleak, though she strove to be fair. "I suppose you have to, for old times' sake. It's just that I've had such a grisly week being interrogated four times by the police. I

35

begin to wish I'd never poked my nose in and owned up about the man dashing in front of my car. How long did I see him? Five seconds at the most, in a thunderstorm with the rain pouring down faster than the wipers could clear it. And they won't believe I can't pick him out from their pictures. They act as though I was a guilty party or something."

"They couldn't think that," Elaine soothed. "According to Robert they're still without a definite lead, so I imagine they're grasping at straws."

"Now they've got me in such a muddle, if he stood a yard from me, I wouldn't recognise him. I can't remember him from Adam. You don't think Martin will start quizzing me?"

"I'm sure he won't."

"What sort of a state is he in?"

"Over the worst of the shock. Don't worry, he won't break down over lunch. I doubt if he'll want to talk about it."

"What's he like?" Rosie asked, cheering up.

Elaine found herself completely lost for an answer. It was as though she was being asked to describe herself. "You'll see. He should be here in half an hour."

Rosie's look sharpened. "When you were kids you and he must have known one another pretty well?"

"Yes. Mrs Ellis was marvellous to me and Dad when Mother died. I was only five, and I don't know how he would have coped without her."

The doorbell rang. Rosie giggled. "Robert! He can't wait to get inside."

He'd brought a bottle of wine which, unwrapped, he presented to Elaine. "I seem to be abominably early. Am I a nuisance?"

From the dining-room door Rosie teased. "You can't keep away. You wouldn't like to fill the interval before lunch by running your masculine eye over the design for my wedding gown, would you?"

"I'd hate to, but I'll probably find myself coerced into doing it."

"Not until you've both had a drink," Elaine insisted. "You

36

pour out, Robert. Give me a glass of sherry. I'll have to take it into the kitchen and leave you to entertain one another for ten minutes."

Robert handing Elaine the glass, opening the door for her, slid one of his professionally penetrating glances into her face. The severely cut leaf-green linen dress, the gloss on her hair, the more than usual care with which she'd made-up her face, plus what he could have sworn was a slow burn of expectation, sounded an alarm bell in his head.

When Elaine was out of earshot, Rosie leaned forward. "We're to have company. Elaine has invited Martin Ellis, you know, old Mr Ellis's son, taken pity on him. I wish she hadn't. It may sound heartless but I'd love a rest from The Murder for one day. You can't say hello to anyone in the street but they start talking about it. And all that police badgering! You know in some ways they are pigs."

"If the man who ran in front of your car had any connection with it, you could be a prime witness." He had spoken abstractedly while he looked through the window at the dead house with the 3-litre Rover standing by the curb.

For a moment Rosie sipped, watching him, then, on the spur of the moment she decided to prod him into action. "Isn't it about time you and Elaine got moving? You've been going around together for a year. If you go on much longer, you won't be able to kick the habit. Honestly, I've seen that happen to scores of couples. They get stuck in a comfortable rut and get too cautious to climb out of it."

"Me, cautious!"

"Her too. Super cautious." She asked in a gentler tone: "Have you seen your little boy recently?"

"No. The last visit didn't work out. You can't expect a child of six to come to terms with divorce: Daddy zooming into his life three times a year, with an armful of presents and a hundred questions because they've become strangers to one another."

She looked sympathetic. "It must be hell. Your ex-wife hasn't married again?"

"No," he snapped and then grinned quickly to show there was no ill-feeling. "Tell me about Bruce. Has he shot any guerillas lately?"

"You know perfectly well he doesn't shoot anyone. His job is maintaining law and order."

He laughed aloud. "Never a bullet fired in anger, let alone self-defence!"

"The Sheik's not a savage. He was educated at Eton!"

"You don't say!"

She glared at him. "That joke was in very poor taste. You owe me an apology, but since I haven't a hope of getting one, you better give me the lowdown on the local scandal. Is it true that Hodgson is going to be asked to resign from the Council because he took a rake-off from the builders of the Parkway Estate?"

She was no better informed on the issue when he'd finished his "inside" story, which had been his precise intention.

Martin checked the arrival of the other two guests from the attic window. A fetching little blonde in a miniskirt and a youngish man with a bottle of wine tucked under his arm. He couldn't place either, which, after an absence of eight years, wasn't surprising, but he found them, viewed in relation to Elaine, an unlikely couple of guests.

The invitation had been for 12:30. He did not stir from his watching-post until 12:45 and then leisurely washed his hands, brushed his jacket.

"Sorry I'm late," he lied, when Elaine opened the door, "but I got caught up in a long telephone call from London."

"Not to worry. It's not the sort of meal that has to be eaten to a deadline. Come and meet the others."

Out of respect for the recently bereaved, Rosie made a half-gesture of rising, gravely held out her hand. She was instantly reassured by Martin's appearance. His face was pleasant, he had a certain amount of style, and if he was bowed down by grief he didn't make a public show of it.

Robert said: "Hello, since I've been asked to act as barman, what will you have?"

"Thanks. A gin and tonic."

Elaine said: "Robert is the chief reporter on the *Evening Argus*."

Martin flicked a sideways glance at him. "Interesting job."

Robert handed Martin his glass, noting the curious matching hair and eyes and that the latter flicked from object to object, suggesting his nerves weren't as steady as he would have you believe. "Sometimes it is; sometimes it's deadly dull."

"And I," Rosie offered, "am a nurse at the General. Since last July State Registered."

"I don't believe it." Automatically Martin smiled admiration into her eyes and perched on the sofa beside her. "More likely to be a first-year probationer."

"Golly, no! The bedpan run is years behind me."

There was no reason why Elaine should not have stayed to have her drink, except that she had a sense of stifling. In the kitchen she drew a few deep breaths, then opened the door wide, stood looking deep into the garden. It was a trancelike state in which she lost track of time. When it lifted she glanced in alarm at her watch. Only five minutes had passed but suddenly the day that was no more than half-worn out, seemed to have lasted an eternity.

She strained the vegetables, put them to keep warm, then with a nervous fumbling gesture opened a drawer in the dresser, burrowed with her fingers under a pile of dusters. When the door opened, she snatched them out.

With slanted head Robert's blue eyes regarded her quizzically. "Did I make you jump? I'm sorry. I just wondered how you were. So how are you?"

It was an odd habit of his never to ask her on first meeting but later, maybe an hour or so, as though introducing a subject of importance.

"I'm fine. You got your car back?"

He nodded. "So I was wondering how you'd like a run over the moors this evening and a drink at The Pelican?" He gave her his warmest, most enticing grin, which was slightly lopsided. "You never know, we might catch a sunset."

"Thanks, Robert, but I don't think so."

With Elaine you had to ask. "Why?"

"I'm going to help Martin sort out some of his mother's clothes that are still hanging up in the wardrobes."

"Is he in *that* much of a hurry to get back to London?"

"He has a job there."

"What's he do?"

"He's the manager of an hotel."

He'd guessed some sort of salesman, or maybe a middle-grade office job. Allowing for prejudice—and Robert Downes was scrupulously honest—superficially Martin Ellis appeared harmless and pleasant-mannered. Not much weight to him, but no big counts against him except what Drummond had deliberately leaked into his ear: eight years ago he had jilted Elaine Lowther and bolted from the town with fifty pounds of stolen money. Whatever he was now, he'd once been a thief.

He came a step closer to her, his voice pleading as it rarely did. "Help him with his rummaging this afternoon. Come out with me this evening. From you I usually take no for an answer and don't argue, but this time, I'm prepared to."

She looked down at her hands then up into his face, at war with herself, not prepared, even for him, to squander time that might be precious.

"Please, Elaine."

"All right, as long as it's not too early."

"Eight? I'll forfeit the sunset. Probably isn't going to be one anyway."

Elaine and Rosie sat opposite one another, the two men in between. Rosie, under a permanent compulsion to talk about Bruce, kept the conversation pivoting round the Sheikdom that would provide her with her nuptial home, plus the visit of her parents to her brother who had settled in Vancouver.

Martin had spent a year in Canada, and was willing to air his knowledge of its climate, scenery, and general amenities, comparing them with those in South Africa.

Robert listened, eyes moving from one to the other, until Rosie teased: "What about your travels?"

"Soon told. Glasgow, Barnsley, London, and Coldbridge."

"But you must have taken some holidays?"

"Camping in the Wye Valley in the days of my far-distant youth, climbing the Cairngorms in my old age, plus a few spells of hard labour chasing film stars, defectors to the West and indiscreet Cabinet Ministers over large tracts of Europe."

"You've no sense of adventure," she scolded, giving him up, and then pleaded with the two men to lend support to her proposal that Elaine should take a spring holiday and spend it lapped in luxury on the Persian Gulf. Elaine admitted it sounded a wonderful idea, but took care not to commit herself.

During the hour they spent over lunch, the word murder was never once spoken aloud. No one alluded to the fact that precisely one week ago Martin Ellis's father had been found foully and brutally beaten to death in the house facing them across the road. Robert found that curious. Granted it was a subject that called for a delicate approach, but surely not a blind-eyed pretence that it had never happened! Or had Martin Ellis and Elaine already talked it dry?

He thought, not for the first time, that Elaine was at her best acting as hostess—the habit of retreating within herself in abeyance, all her attention concentrated on ensuring that each of her guests was at ease and well fed. She was concerned because he refused a second helping of beef. He excused himself on the score of a late breakfast, though Miss Letchworth, as usual, had served it the moment the grandfather clock in the hall broke into its first 9 o'clock chime.

The truth was that somewhere in the last hour he'd lost his appetite.

When they'd finished the cheese, Elaine suggested they had coffee on the terrace. It was sheltered from the wind and with the sun breathing on them, it should be pleasantly warm. But no sooner were they seated than the sun disappeared behind a bank of cloud and the wind spitefully changed direction. It whipped Rosie's miniskirt, cooled the coffee.

At half-past two, Robert was bored with trying to come to terms with a situation he found infuriatingly baffling. Put simply, he could not guess what the hell was going on between Elaine and Martin, even whether there was anything at all. Abruptly he got to his feet, said to Elaine: "The offer you invariably turn down, still holds good. I'll dry while you wash."

Martin looked startled at the suggestion.

Elaine laughed and refused. Rosie, too, offered to help, but not too vehemently. She was due on night duty at eight, and fancied a nap in the afternoon.

Martin rose. "And it's high time I got back to my chores."

Elaine said jerkily, almost nervously: "Could you wait a minute, there's something I want to give you?"

There was an embarrassed pause before Robert and Rosie absorbed the fact that whatever the gift, it was not going to be handed over in their presence.

As Elaine went with them to the door, Martin stood transfixed, hope exploding. Had she changed her mind? If he said he was prepared to accept the money, was she here and now about to make him a present of a cheque for a thousand pounds? He looked about him for confirmation of her financial status. Despite the old-fashioned furniture, there was a sniff of solid prosperity supported by the size and quality of the sirloin and the variety of drink on offer.

When the front door closed, he heard Elaine go directly to the kitchen. A blaze of light began to expand in his head and, when he saw her enter the sitting room, he advanced smiling through the French window to meet her. No slip of paper was visible in her hand, but her fingers were curved over some small object. Despair that came to life in him as quickly and as fiercely as hope pounced.

She uncurved her fingers and held out her palm. On it rested a small leather box rubbed at the corners. It could only hold a ring.

"Engagement rings should be returned when the engagement is broken off. But this one might have chased you halfway round the world and never reached you. I wanted to give it to your mother, but she wouldn't accept it."

The memory that she had not only been his detested nemesis, dogging his heels, threatening his future, but an officially designated fiancée, scorched him with hate. He could not remember what the ring was like, only that it was an old one of his mother's she'd had reset. "It's about time," she insisted in her syrup-sweet but stubborn voice, "that dear little Elaine has a ring."

He made a hoarse protest. "It's a lifetime ago. You don't have to return it."

"But I do. You probably can't remember giving it to me." Her mouth curved in a smile with which he was all too familiar, unnerving him still further. "After all, it was your mother's idea, wasn't it? She bullied you into it." She pressed open the lid.

A square-cut emerald flashed in his eyes. In a purely reflex action his hand reached out and she placed the box in it.

He examined its quality in one swift glance. With luck it should fetch a hundred pounds. He looked up, suddenly pierced by anxiety about the past because of the pattern it imposed upon the present. "Do you still bear me a grudge? Naturally, you did at the time, but how about now?"

She gave a small laugh of derision. "I'd be a neurotic, wouldn't I, if I cherished a grudge against you for eight years!"

Since he was capable of cherishing a grudge against her as long as breath was in his body, the statement carried little conviction, but he was so eager to believe his ears that he accepted she'd wiped her slate clean, and heard himself say: "Maybe if Mum hadn't pushed so hard, it would have come about naturally. You and me, I mean."

Her deep-grey glance was so quietly speculative that the false words that had bounced so cravenly off his tongue frightened him, and he longed to forswear them. "But you wouldn't have stayed in Coldbridge, would you? The only way you could escape was to bolt, wasn't it?"

He nodded.

She looked away from him and after a moment's silence, asked: "Would you like me to give you a hand sorting out your mother's clothes? Your father could never bring himself to let me do it for him. There's a charity jumble sale coming up, and that would be the best way of disposing of them."

Not likely! The distrust and crippling fear she evoked in him, even with the gap of eight years, made her presence a moment longer than necessary obnoxious. "Thanks, but I stayed up working until after midnight, so I intend to take a couple of hours off this afternoon." He left a space for her to ask him for his decision about the thousand pounds and, when she did not mention it, found his nerves were too unsteady for him to do so in a manner that would not betray his desperate need. He added: "I've a date this evening and then I'll get down to another long session of clearing-out tomorrow."

She watched him cross to his own side of the road, saw him run his fingers over the bonnet of the Rover, as if he needed to confirm it was still there. A picture flashed through her head of Mrs Ellis pressing a pound note into his hand as a bribe to take her to a cinema, and she marvelled how abject, yet how relentlessly unassailable, her love had been.

He hadn't mentioned the thousand pounds, which suggested he didn't need it—though remembering the Martin of eight years ago she found that past belief.

When he disappeared behind his own front door, she closed hers. She wondered who his date was with, and instantly banished the query from mind, ashamed of petty curiosity. It was wholly irrelevant to the main issue, suggesting she was suffering a twinge of jealousy, which she most certainly was not.

FIVE

During the course of the afternoon, anticipation of his visit to Sheila gradually erased the chill, mind-clogging memory of Elaine. He persuaded himself that the spasms of fear she jerked alive in him were a throwback to his youth when he had come near to being destroyed by two women, one young, one old, who were hell-bent by sweet talk and inexorable pressure on taking over his life. In retrospect his failure to put up a fight against them reduced him to such a pitiful figure, he thrust the image out of his mind. Those days were dead. He was a man with a firm life pattern now, and if Elaine were fool enough to make him a gift of a thousand pounds, beyond thanks, there was no payment she could wring out of him. But had she any intention of giving him the money? Or was the offer phony, no more than a last desperate stratagem to buy him?

As the day shortened towards twilight his inner ear heard the teasing note in Sheila's husky voice, and across his eye floated that artlessly sensual glance, quickening his impatience and excitement.

He timed his arrival for eight, and was turning into Birch Grove at five minutes to the hour. When he'd been vaguely aware of its existence it had been an area of scrubland that only attracted attention in May when it was carpeted with bluebells. Now a semicircle of road had been driven through it on a lower level than the dozen houses that were screened from each other by professional landscaping. A board informed the public that it was a Private Road with no exit.

The drive to No. 3 climbed between low stone walls. At the top there was a paved courtyard with two garages and standing room for half a dozen cars. He just managed to squeeze the Rover in. Gazing speculatively at the substantial split-level house he estimated its cost at £20,000. How in God's name had Sheila Clark from a mucky back street come to be its mistress?

He rang the bell, then turned to gaze down the spot-lighted terraces of graduated shrubs. The door opened so silently that Sheila's voice made him jump. "Hello, there! I was beginning to wonder if you'd changed your mind. Come on in."

She was wearing a cream trouser suit, her rich auburn hair scooped up on the crown of her head except for two straying half-curled tendrils that caressed her jawline. She held out her hand in a welcoming gesture.

As he took it, felt its silky texture, a sudden and unexpected charge of excitement shot through him. It was at that precise moment it stopped being a game. He wanted her.

He murmured as he followed at her heels along a carpeted hall: "You have a very handsome house."

She looked over her shoulder, so close that he was aware of the creamy, unblemished skin, the freckles of light in her eyes that either deliberately promised or were too innocent to know the light of promise was there. "Thank you. By the way, I wondered if it would be easier on you if I just introduced you as Martin, left out your surname? It's all very informal. I don't suppose you want to talk about it endlessly . . . or don't you mind? You say."

He smiled a gratitude that was genuine. "I don't. I try not to dwell on it more than I can help, but it's damned hard. And I certainly don't want to chat about it at a party."

The room into which she led him was a large oblong with four floor-to-ceiling windows that looked out on to a lighted terrace that afforded a glimpse of a pool at a lower level. His instant assessment told him that it was overrigidly designed and assembled; acquired in a piece from one store, the "antiques" expensive reproductions, the books in the alcove bought by the yard. But he was too tantalised by the evidence of money to deride what his eyes registered. There were around fifteen guests of assorted age groups, ranging from an ancient old bird in a wheelchair, down to a couple of soulful teenagers holding hands.

Sheila raised her voice above the hum of conversation and the stereo music: "Desmond!"

The shortest of three men alongside a drinks table turned and came towards them, his hand poking out in anticipation of a handshake. The suggestion of muscle under his off-the-peg suit, the purposeful upright bearing, saved him from being tubby, but only just. Desmond Bostock's appearance was so ordinary, so unmemorable that you could have met his double down any High Street. Sallow-skinned, near-black short-back-and-sides hair, his wide mouth in a lumpy face was stretched to its limit by a mammoth smile of good-will. Martin was reminded of a toad.

"Desmond, this is Martin. You remember I told you he might be looking in."

Desmond seized Martin's hand, pumped it. "Glad you could make it, Martin." The smile vanished, and he tuned his voice to a sepulchral note. "You've got our sympathy. Terrible . . . for you I mean. Anything we can do, you've only to say. That's what friends are for to stand by in times of grief, and any friend of Sheila's is mine too." He paused, cleared his throat, before enquiring in his ordinary, rather flat voice: "Now, what about a drink?"

The drinks table was well stocked. Martin chose Scotch. Desmond brought back with him a young man as boringly ordinary as himself. "Cliff, Martin. Martin's from London and Cliff's just back from climbing the Dolomites." He cast a paternal look on the soulful teenagers. "And this is Sue, the star of my Drama Club, with Michael, who's a bit of a lay-about. But Sue's going to reform him, aren't you, Sue?"

He swung his glance to Martin, winked. "They've been engaged twenty-five hours. So let's have another toast."

The others raised glasses of Coke as Martin held out his Scotch. Cliff, ignoring Martin, began to urge the teenagers to spend their honeymoon in the Dolomites, leaving Martin's glance free to seek out Sheila. She was talking to a late arrival: a young man who immediately struck him as being of a different calibre from the other mediocre guests. Tall, blond, somewhere in his late twenties, with an air of sophistication, who was leaning his handsome profile far too near Sheila's.

"Desmond," she called. "What do you think, Peter's only come to say he can't stay. He's got to . . ."

The rest of the sentence was rendered inaudible when the old bird manoeuvred her wheelchair alongside him. "You won't remember me, Mr Ellis, but I knew your mother. When she was chairman of the Women's Guild, I was her secretary. You would have been sixteen or seventeen." Her hard bitter little eyes expressed contempt. "You haven't changed all that much. She fretted for you, you know. She was fretting for you when I visited her the day before she died."

So much for Sheila's attempt to shield him from the stings of gossip! Probably everyone in the room was getting a macabre kick out of slyly observing the behaviour of a son whose father had been murdered! He was saved from concocting excuses by the arrival at their side of a clergyman who began to expatiate at length on a festival of music he was proposing to produce in the nave of his church.

Martin managed a pretence of listening, but in fact the vicar's words floated past his ears. With the exception of the unknown Peter who'd departed in the act of arriving, all the guests struck him as stupefyingly dull: either conventional couples rooted well into middle-age or near-dumb offshoots of Desmond's schoolteaching. Why, with her looks, style, plus the background of a fine house, did Sheila choose to act as hostess to such a boring collection of human beings? The slick answer was that they were Desmond's friends. But why was she willing to waste her energy and assets on such people? Because he gave her no choice? Was the glad-handing Desmond a pocket dictator in his own home?

Relief arrived when Sheila appeared in a gap between two sliding doors leading into the dining room. "What do you say we eat?"

She beckoned her guests towards a buffet supper spread on a refectory table: cold salmon, turkey, a ham, bowls of salad, an excellent cheeseboard, and fresh raspberries flanked by a pitcher of cream.

Martin hung back in order to be the last one in, whispered: "I wish I were a starving man. How much do you pay the *cordon bleu* chef you've got hidden away in the kitchen?"

She laughed under her breath. "I don't employ one. But I've got a super delicatessen. It's more reliable and it doesn't fly into tantrums."

During supper he was sandwiched between a grey-haired spinster given to giggling and making artless jokes, who played the violin in the vicar's orchestra, and the soulful, near dumb teenagers. He escaped as soon as his plate was empty.

When Sheila had finished pouring the coffee, she came and sat beside his chair. "We haven't had much opportunity to talk about old times, have we?"

"Do you want to?" he challenged. "Were they even good enough to remember, let alone reminisce about?"

"Oh, you mean Granddad! He went for all my boy friends with a broom; it was his way of testing their manhood." She brushed a speck of cigarette ash off her cream suit. "You failed the test, never showed up again." She looked at him under her lashes, smiled to take away the sting of reproach. "He was a heavyweight boxer when he was young, so only another boxer stood an earthly chance against him."

"Thanks for the crumb of comfort. Do you do this every

Sunday, keep open house for your friends, feed them on fresh salmon and cold turkey?"

"The menu varies, but most Sundays." She swung her glance slowly about the room, resting it on the furniture, silk curtains, the great bowls of flowers, her expression inimical except that she was not displeased with what she saw. Deliberately he made no attempt to break the silence but used it as pressure to induce her to speak. After all, he could hardly say: Where did you get the money to buy all this? He refused to credit that her lump of a husband who, with his sickening act of brotherly love towards all men became less prepossessing with every passing moment, had provided it. Yet where else could it have come from?

When she spoke it was only to say: "If you're still here next Sunday, come again."

"Two suppers in a row!" He shook his head in flat denial. "Which I can't return: an empty house, no cook, a rundown, dilapidated kitchen! Even if I could spy out your delicatessen, I couldn't put on a decent meal." He watched her down-bent head as she tinkled a silver spoon against her coffee cup. "A much better idea would be if you could both have a meal out with me some evening."

"Desmond has such a host of after-school activities in term-time, he hardly ever has a free evening."

His spirits zoomed. The message could not have been plainer. "Then what about having lunch with me. Any chance of your managing that?"

"I might." She slanted her face towards him, the intriguing specks of mischief glinting in her eyes, murmured: "Give me a ring and we'll see."

The party broke up as soon as Sheila had made her last round with the coffee, at what to Martin seemed an ungodly hour. The first guest to say goodbye was a stout, baldheaded man, with a puffball-shaped wife, both of whom had been shocked and at a loss for conversation when they'd learnt Martin didn't play golf. They set off a chain reaction. The other guests began to look at their watches, murmur that

Monday was a working day, and make their adieux. In the general handshaking Desmond Bostock gripped Martin's fist. "I'm so glad you could make it, Martin. Now you know where we live, we'll expect to see you again. In a time of trial such as you're going through, both Sheila and I want to help all we can. So do us the favour of asking."

What was he, Martin asked himself, solid wood from the neck up, or so damned vain and cocky he didn't recognise the manner in which other men eyed his wife? That fellow Peter, for instance.

By ten-thirty Martin was home, not a single question answered, the speculations creating an area of turmoil in his head. In the interval before sleep, the squat, glad-handing, patronising Desmond became more and more to resemble a toad.

Ordering a third round of drinks, Robert decided, not for the first time, that it was all wasted effort. Why, in heaven's name, did he pursue a girl whose reactions and responses were no more than skin deep, mere shadows of the heart? For once, he spoke out his thoughts. "I never really get through to you, do I?"

Elaine's glance seemed to quiver. "What do you mean?"

"Oh, come on, while you've been drinking, you've been light-years away. All I have is a shell of a girl who makes all the right answers. A darling talking doll!"

She had no defence, was honest enough not to concoct one. "Then why ask me out?"

"In the hope that one day you'll tell me where you go; where, for instance, you are right this minute?"

"Right now, I'm with you."

"Only because I jogged your arm." She baffled, enthralled, and defeated him. In theory her life should have been an open book: responsible job, impeccable if dull home background, all the correct hobbies and community interests; no visible male commitments. Granted that in certain lights she possessed the particular type of restrained beauty

53

that intrigued him, but he'd known quite a few such girls—including his ex-wife—and won or lost them with no permanent scars on the heart. So why the devil couldn't he bring himself to leave Elaine to dream unmolested in whatever limbo she retreated to? The answer could only be that she posed a challenge to his vanity. When he went back to Fleet Street—and, astounding him, the decision to do so cohered at that instant—he'd seen himself taking Elaine with him. Suddenly he laughed aloud.

She looked puzzled. "What's funny?"

"You. Funny and impossible." He decided he'd given her enough leeway. "Now tell me about Martin Ellis."

"You met him at lunch. You know his background, why he's here . . ." Her voice trailed away, died.

The question had really been what she was prepared to tell him. He'd got his answer: nothing. Neither the theft nor the jilting, an omission that revealed facts he'd rather not have known. He pressed: "You and he, as kids, teenagers, must have known one another pretty well?"

She met and held his glance for a moment, then accused: "You've been asking questions, reporters' questions, and someone has told you that Martin and I were once engaged to be married."

He nodded, waiting.

"The engagement ended when he drove a car a businessman wanted delivered to his villa in Italy. For company he took along a girl I knew." Before he could frame a comment, she went on quickly, looking down at her glass to shield her gaze from his: "And if you're about to ask me how I reacted, it wouldn't serve any useful purpose. It happened so long ago, I honestly can't remember. It belongs to a different time zone."

He wanted to believe her, but belief remained dead. Also she hadn't mentioned the theft. "But you feed and entertain him?"

"My relationship with the family wasn't restricted to Martin. His parents, particularly his mother, showed me

54

untold kindness and affection when my own mother died when I was five. I feed him as much for their sakes as his own."

A reasoned defence, but to his ears it suggested a loyalty still wholly committed. He pressed: "But he never once came back to see them during eight years?"

"That's true. And it hurt them, but to do him justice he was too busy spinning round the world, at least until fairly recently." She drew a circle on the table with her fingernail. "Who did you ask about Martin and me?"

"I didn't ask anyone. Someone told me."

"Who?"

"Chief Superintendent Drummond. He mentioned Martin to me."

In a reflex action her glance came up, wide, startled. "In what connection?"

"Purely as next of kin. That they'd at last managed to make contact with him." He eyed her sardonically. "There's a murder hunt on, love. A large number of the County as well as the Coldbridge police are involved. Everyone remotely connected with Mervyn Ellis is being what is called processed."

"I know that. Who better! What I didn't realise was that police superintendents gossiped."

"Everyone gossips. It's part of the makeup of the entire human race. Furthermore, it's inevitable that the next of kin are put through a hair sieve. A high proportion of murders are committed by the victim's nearest and dearest."

A look of blank shock shuttered her eyes. "Was that meant to be a joke?"

Contrite that he'd upset her, he apologised. "Sorry. Probably, in the circumstances, one in doubtful taste. As far as I know, Martin Ellis is not under the faintest suspicion of murdering his father."

On the half hour's drive back to Coldbridge he was at pains to divert her and restore her spirits. She was, as ever, sensitive to his kindness, and strained to respond, but she

55

couldn't quite force herself far enough. She said when they reached her house: "I'm a drag, but I don't mean to be."

"Something clicks or it doesn't. It's as simple as that. Tonight just wasn't our night. I think, though I wouldn't swear to it, that I'm grateful to you for being honest. You can't say I don't try."

"You could give up."

"That had crossed my mind. Maybe I will . . . one day."

He saw her to the door but made no attempt to kiss her; nor did he ask her for another date. Driving home he worked on the enigma and came up with one possible answer: she was waiting for something or someone, meanwhile existing in a state of suspension. Martin Ellis? For God's sake, did any modern woman remain fast in love for eight years with a totally unremarkable young man who'd jilted her, and was a thief to boot? Not if she wasn't crazy. And that Elaine was even to the smallest degree unbalanced he was not yet prepared to admit. It remained no more than an ugly shadow on the outer fringes of his mind.

SIX

At half-past eight on Monday morning Amos Branding, proprietor of a secondhand jewellery and pawnshop in Manchester, telephoned his local police station. Within minutes the information he supplied was relayed to the operations room at Coldbridge Headquarters.

Naylor studied the teleprint. On Friday afternoon, shortly before closing time, a youth had come in offering for sale a pair of solid silver candlesticks and a cigarette box. Amos Branding, recovering from flu, had been coddling himself in bed, and the transaction had been handled by his assistant Herbert Tilson, who had bought them from the youth for the sum of £37.50. Asked his name for the recipt he had given it as George Blake. On Sunday evening Amos Branding had been sufficiently himself to stagger into his shop, where he studied the police lists of stolen property. As a law-abiding citizen he had immediately contacted his local headquarters.

"George Blake!" Naylor growled.

"One of the fun brigade!" Sergeant Tanner sniggered, and instantly regretted it. Naylor's meagre sense of humour was in cold storage. He ordered a squad car to proceed at speed to collect Mr Branding, his assistant, and the stolen silver.

Amos Branding was a pallid, desiccated man in his sixties, at once nervous and ingratiating. His young assistant was divided between excitement at finding himself in the limelight and apprehension about the end result.

Naylor eyed them both with disfavour. "You normally

purchase valuable articles of silver from youths without enquiring how they came by them?"

"Most certainly not," Branding retorted, who was nothing if not a chancer—but not in a murder case. "My assistant enquired how he'd acquired them, didn't you, Herbert?"

"Yes, sir." Herbert swallowed. "He said they had been his mother's, who died two years ago. He didn't want to part with them, but now he was unemployed and needed the money."

"Thirty-seven pounds, fifty pence. Solid silver, the candlesticks Georgian. At a conservative estimate they were worth over two hundred pounds. It was a fence's price and you know it, so don't let's argue that one out." He turned to Herbert, who was growing paler by the second. "Now from you, my lad, I want every single detail you can remember about the youth who sold you the stolen articles. So rattle your brains."

Herbert was made to repeat his description a dozen times. About eighteen to twenty. Fair shoulder-length hair, a bit curly. A face that was beyond Herbert's ability to describe, but he was medium tall, just about Herbert's own height, and thin. He'd been wearing a navy-blue anorak, jeans, and he took the silver out of a rucksack he'd got slung across his shoulder.

No amount of coercion could prise a more satisfactory description out of the now perspiring Herbert. He recognised no photograph that was put under his nose.

Branding pleaded in defence of his assistant: "You see, Inspector, you don't expect to have to give a detailed description of every customer."

"You should have expected to have had to describe this one, even to count his eyelashes," Naylor retorted.

Master and employee were being escorted back to the squad car when Herbert's memory sparked into action, and he did a fast lope back to Naylor's office. "He wore a ring," he stuttered in triumph. "I knew there was something about him, but it wouldn't come back to me. A ring on his left hand, bronze or dark gold, nearly brown really, not solid, but sort of filigree, a big one that reached his first knuckle." He waited for praise. None was forthcoming.

"Two a penny," Drummond remarked cynically. "Every dropout, hippie, clerk, or shop assistant under thirty on his day off is dripping with chains, beads, bangles, and rings."

"As you say," Naylor conceded, "but I'm certain I've seen a ring that fits the description. Fair time ago but not all that long." He knew it would come to him if he didn't chase it. When it did, it was 2 A.M. on Tuesday morning. Soon after eight he was knocking on the door of 10, Kenilworth Court, one of Coldbridge's earlier blocks of high-rise flats.

Elsie Ramsgate opened it, already neatly hatted and coated for work. She was forty-five and looked every day of her age. Her premature silver hair that had once been blond would have been an asset if she hadn't dragged it back from her forehead and screwed it into a tight ball in her neck. She still retained the remnants of a fine complexion, but her face was pinched, with pleats of wrinkles across her brow, and a tense expression in her blue eyes that betrayed a permanent inward tick of apprehension. She weighed slightly under eight stone.

Naylor had first come to know her ten months ago and was acquainted with her history. A lone fearless battler, she commanded his respect, and he spoke with more courtesy than the occasion warranted. "Good morning, Elsie. May I come in?"

She stood stiffly back. "Not much good my saying no, is it?"

"No reason why you should. I shan't keep you long."

The kitchen into which she led him was spanking clean, the floor still damp from its recent scrub. Elsie Ramsgate worked an eight-hour day five and a half days a week in a supermarket. In the evenings she knitted garments for private customers, sometimes baby-sat while she did so. She was a woman who did not squander a minute of time that could be turned into money. Her reward was she didn't owe a penny, and next year's rent was already safe in the Post Office. She could have afforded to work less, but the compulsion to win herself a wider margin of security that had driven her for over eighteen years had become a life force.

"I suppose," Naylor suggested, "Tony's not up yet?"

"He's gone to stay with his Auntie Maggie in Manchester, Wythenshawe." She paused, alarm gathering within her. "What do you want him for? He's done nothing, that I can swear. Ask his probation officer, Mr Wells, if you don't believe me."

"No job yet?"

"There aren't any jobs for teenagers. That's why they're all hanging round street corners. You should know that!"

"And getting into mischief."

"What mischief is Tony supposed to have got into? That's why you're here, isn't it?"

"He sold some silver that didn't belong to him."

She swore as solemnly as if her hand was on a Bible: "He's never stolen a thing in his life."

"Elsie! He once tried to steal a car, as you well know."

"That's your story. He'd never have driven it away."

"Well, we'll never know that for certain, will we? When did he go to his Auntie Maggie's?"

"A bit over a week ago."

"Why did he go?"

"He's got a friend who'd been taken on at a box-making factory not far from her flat, and he said there might be other jobs going. He never lets up trying to get work."

"What day did he go to his Auntie Maggie's?"

"Last Sunday week."

"Then I'll be wanting his Auntie Maggie's address."

"If he didn't get taken on at the factory, he'll have left by now, probably be on his way home."

Naylor's voice hardened. "Elsie, he's got to be found. Today. He sold two solid silver candlesticks and a cigarette box that didn't belong to him."

Elsie Ramsgate's skin wasn't the type that paled under

60

shock, it merely drew tighter over her bones until her face looked like that of an old woman. Grinding fear and blazing outrage quelled her voice to a whisper. "Do you think I'm daft! What you're talking about is the three bits of silver stolen from that old man who was clubbed to death. Well, Tony didn't steal them. And as for killing anyone, you must be clean out of your mind. He's against violence, and if he's got any religion it's something from India called Buddhism. It doesn't allow you to kill a fly. He won't let me have a mousetrap in the flat and half the time I can't get him to swallow a morsel of meat. You're on the wrong track this time, Mr Naylor, that you are."

"I hope I am. Now let's have your sister's address."

She dictated it to him, then turned her back and refused to utter another syllable. Elsie Ramsgate was a woman without friends or confidants—she hadn't time to cultivate them. All the love of which she was capable was spent upon her son. The security she slaved for was to protect him—from what she never put into thought much less words. Standing ramrod straight, a terrorising memory surfaced: of Tony heaving his heart out in the bathroom at 2 A.M. on that Sunday morning, tears pouring down his cheeks, grey-faced and rigid with shock.

Maggie Trench bore no resemblance to her sister. She was fat, good-natured, had been married twice and had forsworn husbands for friendly lodgers who came and went from her colourfully furnished Council flat. She had two daughters who, in twenty-two and twenty-three years' time, would be exact replicas of their mother. At the moment, the lodger being a bachelor long-distance lorry driver, the living was easy, and though Maggie had nothing but contempt for her dried-up stick of a sister, she had a soft spot for Tony. When he turned up she bedded him down on a sofa in the living room, served him with the mammoth fry-ups on which she fed the family.

When Naylor arrived Tony had been gone twenty-four

hours. She ogled Naylor out of force of habit, fiddled with her orange fringe. "Now, how would I know where he is if he isn't at home, officer! Off to hitch a lift to somewhere. Could be London, could be Carlisle." She giggled. "Or Timbuctoo. Distance's no object to youngsters today. My Eileen's got a fellow who's just got back from Istanbul, wherever that is."

She was affronted at the very idea that stolen property had been hidden in her house. Tony a thief! Sergeant Naylor must be joking. A gentler, sweeter boy than Tony never breathed. Give his last cent away, he would. Mind you, to her way of thinking, he was too good-natured, but that didn't make him a thief.

Yes, she admitted, he'd come with a rucksack slung over his shoulder, but where else would he keep his spare jeans and the load of books he always carried round with him.

Ten minutes after Naylor bade her a brisk farewell, a general country-wide alert, with a special watch on railway stations, airports, and docks was put out for Anthony James Ramsgate, nineteen years old, height 5′ 10″, thin build, blond shoulder-length hair, blue eyes with dark lashes. When last seen he had been wearing faded blue jeans, white T-shirt, brown sandals and carrying a navy rucksack.

Tony Ramsgate sat in an open barn at Catchhill, five miles from Coldbridge, his head bent deep over his knees, a swimming sensation in his head. Used to house stock in the winter, the barn was littered with bales of hay that, with a little manipulation, made battlements to hide behind. It overlooked gently rolling pastureland where cattle grazed, the farmhouse to which it belonged hidden inside a circle of trees. Far off was the sound of a tractor but not a human being was in sight. He and Juliet had discovered it three months ago, when it had been light until ten o'clock at night, and there had been less panic for her to be home before dark.

He heard a sound, jerked his head upright, but it wasn't

her running step, and before his head subsided he groaned aloud. In the back pocket of his jeans was a painfully accumulated wad of grubby notes that amounted to £139: the price of a single bus ticket to Katmandu, an escape route to a private heaven for two. Juliet, who had booked the tickets with the travel agent, had pleaded to pay for his as well as her own, but that was an ignominy to which he would not submit. But now that, against all odds, he'd finally accumulated the money, would *they* let them catch the bus, sit, their hands locked, as it rolled through Greece, Turkey, Persia, Afghanistan, and Pakistan to within sight of Everest? He began to shake, while that most nauseating of all smells assailed his nostrils.

The sound of her light feet running down the field behind the barn, jerked him upright. Quickly he wiped a hand over his face to obliterate whatever pain was there. He did not move except to hold out his arms and, when she reached him, enclose her tiny, fragile form within them. He kissed every inch of her face, threaded his fingers through her long silk hair that was so pale a yellow that in the shadowy barn it took on an elfin tinge of green, whispered: "I couldn't be sure you'd make it, that you'd get my letter in time."

She leaned back from him, the small triangle of her face, the beautifully shaped blue eyes forever a fresh miracle to him, and whispered back: "Why didn't you tell me you were going away?"

"I heard of a job, suddenly, and went after it. Money for the kitty!"

"But you didn't get it?"

"I did, but it only lasted a week." He kissed the tip of her tip-tilted nose. "Still, it did the trick. Ticket money complete." He handed it to her.

She shook her head, half-cross, half-admiring his touchy pride. "What's it matter whose money it is, yours or mine? It's ours. I wouldn't have fussed if you'd had to pay for my ticket."

"There's nothing to fuss over any more." He kissed her again.

They sat down, close, fingers laced tight together. She spoke with quiet exultancy. "All I have to do now is to dream up a plan to stop Mummy driving me to that grisly finishing school. And then, there you'll be, waiting for me at St Pancras Station. I found out the time the train arrives months ago. Noon. Then we'll get on a bus to Clapham Common, and by night we'll be on the other side of the Channel. Before the school gets round to ringing Mummy to ask why I haven't turned up we'll be halfway to Greece." She threw back her head, so that her hair was airborne, laughed with the unreserved gaiety of a child. "I'm seventeen and there's no power on earth that can drag me back." She leaned her face, grave now, against his. "Remember my promise? We're never going to be unhappy again in our whole lives."

For a whole minute they lay side by side against the giant blocks of hay before she asked: "What did you have to do to earn the last of your ticket money?"

"Sweep a factory floor while the boy who usually did it was on holiday." The lie was like a knife plunging into his side; it made him feel sick. He'd lied all his life to save himself from the ordeal of watching his mother break her heart over him. But today was the first time he'd lied to Juliet.

"Keep your passport safe." She sounded anxious in a bossy maternal way. "And you're sure no one knows you've got it? Not even your mother?"

"It's safe, and no one knows I've got it." But there would be a record at the office where it had been issued to Anthony James Ramsgate. Did they, he wondered, keep a note of names on passports as you crossed frontiers? He said fiercely: "Nothing's going to go wrong."

She looked startled. "I've never imagined anything could go wrong. It can't. What made you say that?"

"Just stating the obvious." He kissed her, pressing her slight body against his own, then brought out with a rush:

"But I don't think we ought to be seen together, not until St Pancras."

"Why?" She looked puzzled, teetering on the verge of hurt and alarm. "Don't you want to, not for two whole weeks?"

"Your dad has eyes at the back of his head. So's my mum, plus a bit of extrasensory perception thrown in." Sometimes it seemed to him she kept him under surveillance twenty-four hours a day, crucifying herself with the idea that he'd drop dead or something. "So no risks, eh?"

"But why can't we see one another here? We don't even come together or leave together." She scanned his face. "You're scared, I can feel you trembling inside. Tell me why. You've got to tell me. We're one. You know we are. We don't keep secrets from each other."

"Not scared," he lied. "I don't want you to have to fight your way out of a great emotional scene. And you might have to if someone saw us together and reported back to your mum or dad. That's what we planned, to slip away, drift out of their lives. Well, isn't it?"

"Yes. But I could handle them." It was a child's boast. She burst out: "I wish to heaven I had six brothers and sisters, then I'd not be their only treasure they keep in a cage."

At least her mum had a husband: his had been deserted when he'd been six months old. Sometimes, but not often, he wondered what his father was like; where he lived, if he'd ever passed him in the street. "They'd put on a great big act of being hurt. That'd tear you up. If you don't see them, you won't have the picture in your mind to make you miserable. That makes sense, darling."

"You being sensible! That'll be the day." She laughed, arching her slender neck. He thought: I'd kill myself before I hurt her. That done, he, too, wouldn't be haunted by the black pictures that were forever slipping in and out of his head.

Reluctantly she gave in. "All right. I'll do it for you, this once." Suddenly tears welled in her eyes, but they didn't brim over her lids. "Two whole weeks," she moaned. "How are you going to spend them?"

"I'll try Scarborough to see if there are any jobs going there. With the season still on, there might be."

"Not at home?"

"No."

She leaned forward, gazing down the pastureland, which she didn't see. "Parents shackle children with love. We'll never do that to ours. When they're thirteen or fourteen we'll say: off with you, go and find a world of your own." She smiled guilelessly at her dream, began to spin another. "Maybe we'll find somewhere to live on the edge of a tea plantation where they'll let us work picking the leaves. Or we could go on to Australia and end up on the Great Barrier Reef. Would you fancy that?"

"I'd prefer the Great Barrier Reef to picking tea leaves!"

"Then we'll make for the Great Barrier Reef." The dream receded, and she looked at him with desolate entreaty. "You'll write to me while you're in Scarborough. You must; I'll die if you don't. I nearly did last week until I got your letter."

"But I won't have an address."

The smile came back to her face as she mocked: "The gaps in your general knowledge are a mile wide. Care of the General Post Office, Scarborough. I shall write tomorrow, so mind you go and pick it up, and write back to me. Promise?"

He promised, a promise he wasn't sure he'd be able to keep. When the fields lost their depth of green, faded into a neutral colour, the dry-stone walls dividing them invisible, they made love.

Drowsily she whispered: "You see, we are one. We'd cease to exist without one another, be nothing-creatures." She buried her head in his shoulder. "Two weeks! I don't think I can live without you that long."

He kissed and caressed her with an urgency that half frightened him. "Yes, you can, and I will write, but letters can get lost, and in case mine does, I want St Pancras, noon, the 4th October written in big caps on your heart."

She gave a little sighing moan. "It's been there for months. Oh, hell, I've got to go or they'll think I've been raped in a ditch. Come as far as the main road with me."

He walked half a mile, to the point where she'd left her bike. Presently, when he'd rehearsed the question in his head half a dozen times, he asked: "What's been going on while I've been away?"

"The same old dreary round! Oh, and there's been a murder, a horrible one. An old man who lived alone in Hartfield Road. Someone broke in and beat him to death."

"Have they caught the murderer?"

"I don't know. I don't think so."

It was nearly dark when there was nowhere else for them to go together. He checked the lamp on the bicycle. She mounted it in a scrambling rush. "I'm not going to say goodbye. I never have to you and I never will."

"Keep safe," he called after her, "please keep safe," but she was too far away to hear him.

SEVEN

When Martin telephoned Sheila early on Monday afternoon to ask her to lunch on Tuesday, he left the choice of eating place to her. She picked the Sligh Pass Hotel, fifteen miles from Coldbridge, a haunt of fishermen and grouse-shooters. Midday, with most of them deployed with their packed lunches along the riverbank or among the heather, the dining room was sparsely occupied by a few non-sporting wives and a handful of day tourists. It was an hotel that cultivated an air of understated comfort, a total disregard of prices, reverential waiters, heavy silver covers, starched napkins and an impressive wine list.

Sheila knew her way about the menu, and was so discriminating in her choice of food and drink that Martin experienced a qualm that he might run short of notes to pay the bill. During lunch he told her that the police had recovered his father's silver, which he'd been called upon to identify, but they hadn't yet caught the thief.

"He must have been the murderer too, mustn't he?"

"Obviously. I saw Superintendent Drummond, and he said, with a bit of luck, they'd have him in custody within the next twenty-four hours."

"The quicker the better for you. I mean, once the trial is over, you'll be able to put it behind you, forget the ghastliness of it all."

He agreed.

Over lunch he was at pains to keep the conversation light, his sole aim being to divert her. Her air of superb physical well-being combined with rich sensual overtones fascinated him. So far as he could judge, she was perfectly happy to be where she was, untroubled in conscience by making a date for lunch which she would not, he'd be prepared to bet, divulge to Desmond. By the time they walked into the courtyard, he considered his patience exemplary, and that the moment had arrived for him to collect a reward.

"What about a private conducted tour of the pass? As a boy scout I once camped on the other side. I can promise not to lose you." He indicated the flawless duck-egg blue sky, the rolling spread of purple heather in the middistance.

She made a little grimace of doubt, glanced down at her shoes. "Provided it's strictly on wheels."

He drove up a dozen corkscrew twists, descended two, then manoeuvred into a makeshift lay-by and cut the engine.

"Listen," she said with innocent delight that might or might not be genuine, "the larks are still singing. Can you hear them?" She gazed at the panorama of overlapping moors. "Last time I was up here it poured in torrents, and the visibility was down to about ten yards."

He leaned back, took a rug from the back seat. "It would be a lot cooler out of the car. Let's climb over the first wall, then we can use it as a back rest."

She flicked her guileless but assured glance over him, then lifted the door catch. She was wearing an oyster-coloured gossamer wool shift dress. She'd already discarded the matching jacket and her arms were bare, softly rounded as a teenager's. Keeping behind her he relished her legs which showed no thickening above the knees, tapered to delicately boned ankles. She turned her head, caught him. He laughed without embarrassment. "You can't blame me for looking."

She answered in the same light tone. "But I'd hate you to get overoptimistic."

He spread the rug against the base of the dry-stone wall, and they smoked a cigarette in silence. It was then that, unheralded, uninvited, the plaguing image of Elaine flashed through his head. He'd braced himself for her appearance —on some pretext or other—on his doorstep on Monday evening. But she hadn't shown up. Her absence, the suspense in which it left him, dragged at his nerves. If she were serious about the thousand pounds, why hadn't she raised the subject on Sunday? Distrust that amounted to a nagging fear, a certainty that she was engaged in some devious act of trickery, filled him with foreboding. The devilish part was that he couldn't be absolutely sure. She had so many quirks and imbalances in her makeup, that the offer just might be genuine. If so, and he could persuade her to advance it within a fortnight, he could use it as a first down payment to Folk.

For relief from the ignominy of feeling himself once again at Elaine's mercy, he let his glance rest on the superlative prize beside him. She answered it with a mocking: "You're so bursting with questions, why don't you ask one?"

"You might tell me to mind my own business."

"Try me! You can only die once."

"What made a beautiful girl like you marry a man like Desmond Bostock for his money?"

She laughed but not in amusement. "When we came out of the registrar's office he had £49 in the bank. Our honeymoon was a week in Keswick with £3 a day to cover the boardinghouse, petrol, and spending money. We came back to a semidetached on Arnford Road with only two rooms furnished and a mortgage hanging round our necks. So, correction, apart from his salary, Desmond hadn't any money for me to marry."

"But he's got a hell of a lot now!"

She stared at the blue pencil curves of the winding river, seeming either not to hear, or not choosing to answer. Her face, reshaped by a new emotion, took on harder lines. When she did speak, it was slowly, but fluently, as though she were repeating an old story. "While we were in Keswick, Granddad had a stroke. When the hospital discharged him, it was either a geriatric Home or coming to live with us. I opted for the Home; Desmond insisted it was our Christian duty to look after him. For ten months we did just that, me during the day, Desmond at night. He was incontinent, he had to be fed, and he rapped his stick all day long on the bedroom floor. Over three hundred days being a slave to a filthy loathsome creature who couldn't keep himself clean for ten minutes. I still have nightmares of spooning food into a mouth that dribbled it out."

"My God! Desmond . . . Why?"

"I told you. His Christian duty. He believes in what he calls the natural order of life. Children are cared for by their parents, and then when the parents are old and helpless, the grown-up children repay the debt. It's a sort of creed with him, one he holds sacred. After the funeral Mr Redditch, the solicitor, asked me to go and see him. I took it for granted it was about Granddad's slummy little house: I thought now we'll be able to sell it and pay off some of the mortgage."

She gave him an odd, tight smile, went on: "But it wasn't. When I was seventeen, serving in Woolworth's, Granddad had won £132,000 on a football pool. He'd put the whole lot, without spending a penny of it, on deposit in a bank. An eccentric, that's how Mr Redditch described him." She laughed, and it wasn't a pretty sound. "What he was was a master-miser to outshine all misers. He couldn't admit he'd got a penny besides his pension because he'd have had to spend some of it on other people. Buy himself a new suit, and I'd have nagged him for warm winter boots. Buy more beer at the pub, and he'd have been expected to stand a round for his mates. So he wore patched pyjamas, an old dressing gown that was only fit for burning. For ten months, when he had a fortune in the bank, he tied me to the filthy job of nursing him. And he got a hell of a lot more kick out of that than spending his money."

She stared down the angles of moorland, her face blenched, taut with hate that momentarily robbed her of beauty. Then she shrugged, though her voice still shook. "That answers your question. The money's not Desmond's, it's mine."

In his head he saw the interwoven pattern of all the dead ends he followed to win money that was a pittance when set against the riches that had fallen into the lap of a common little man he'd despised on sight. He tried to speak, but his voice wouldn't sound.

She smiled commiseratingly. "I know exactly how you feel. It's like something that happens to someone else. But it happened to me, ten months too late."

Now his voice burst into a near-shout. "Because you wouldn't have married Desmond if you'd had a quarter of a million."

"I wouldn't have married anyone."

"Then undo it. It's easy enough now."

"With Desmond? You underrate him. He counts divorce a sin, along with gambling, overindulgence in drink, inheriting unearned wealth."

"He benefits from yours! He lives in a rich man's house, eats food that he couldn't buy on a schoolteacher's salary!"

"Even a saint has a few blind spots. He can't prevent me spending my money. He couldn't stop me buying the house, and having bought it, he had to move in with me. He pays me the same housekeeping allowance as he did at the old semi. When we go out together we go in his car, which is nine years old. When we have a meal out, we eat it in a place that he can afford."

It was a situation so beyond credibility that his mind refused to assimilate it. "There's been a new divorce law for years now. You don't have to prove cruelty, adultery, or what have you, only irretrievable breakdown of a marriage, and even if a husband or wife is unwilling, after five years' separation, the other partner can obtain a divorce. How long did you say you'd been married?"

"That's not the point. Desmond has not deserted me, nor I he."

"He sounds to me like a nut case, or the masculine equivalent of a golddigger."

"He's neither," she said picking her words slowly. "He's good. A Good Man, capital letters. They are pretty rare on the ground."

"So you're going to stay married to him forever?"

"I didn't say that, did I?"

The teasing note had returned to her voice, and her mood had softened, as though she'd temporarily purged her bitterness, and was again the woman who'd walked to his table in The Three Kings. He let his hand fall accidentally on hers. She allowed it to remain. After a moment she turned her head. Her eyes were lazy with heat, and the line of her mouth was languorous, waiting. He caught her savagely, bent his lips over hers, held her hard to him. Her body was compliant, unprotesting as he eased her away from the wall. They lay side by side, the springy heather like a rough couch beneath them. But when his hands grew more demanding, she released herself adeptly. She brushed her dress smooth, seemingly in possession of her emotions, though there was a bead of moisture on her forehead, and her voice was not as uncommitted as she would have him believe. "You're a fast worker, but you can't say I didn't warn you."

He jackknifed forward to hide his disappointment. He'd believed he'd been going to have her, that one claim would be established that afternoon.

She laid a finger on the back of his neck. "Don't be angry. Time's against us. I have to be at Billy Corbett's at four. It's half-past three, and it'll take us a good half an hour to get there."

"Who the hell is Billy Corbett?"

"One of Desmond's good causes. He's blind and lives in a cottage on Ben Tor. Desmond visits him every Thursday night. Last week Billy's transistor packed up, so he brought it away, mended it, and this morning I promised I'd take it back to Billy." She picked up her handbag, jumped lightly to her feet.

He drew her against him, pressed his mouth hard on hers. Her response was adequate but no more. "And talking of husbands, as we were, where do you keep your wife? Snug in London?"

"I'm not married." There'd been one wife in South Africa who had divorced him, nearly a second in Canada.

"That amazes me," she said with genuine surprise.

"If that's meant to be a compliment, thanks."

She made no protest when he lifted her over the low stone wall, kept his arm round her waist until they reached the lay-by. She directed him on a downhill route of side roads, and then up an ascending lane. "There it is. You can see it now."

It was a squat stone cottage, set on the top of a hill grazed by sheep, open to the wind and weather on three sides, shielded on the fourth by a wall.

"Who else lives there besides this blind fellow?"

"No one. Since his mother died a couple of years ago he's lived alone except for his dog. He was born there; his father was a shepherd, and so was Billy until he lost his sight. Because he's never known anywhere else, it's all mapped out in his mind. He goes walking for miles. I suppose Scout, his dog, helps. Stop the car in the lane by that gate. There's no way up to the cottage except on foot." She reached for the radio. "I won't be long. Ten minutes . . . about."

"I'll come with you."

"No, don't. Strangers upset him. He's terrified that they might be from the Welfare Department trying to edge him into a Home for the Blind. Last winter he was snowed up for ten days and there was a lot of talk about it not being safe for him to be so isolated. And he won't have a telephone."

He watched her climb the steep sheep track, and when she disappeared inside the cottage, he walked towards the stone wall. Leaning over it, he could see, lying deep in the valley, a sizeable house surrounded by gardens, an orchard, with a long drive from the road. Even from that distance it was obviously dilapidated and unoccupied. The grass in the orchard hadn't been cut, and most of the outbuildings appeared to be on the point of collapse.

A spurt of inconsequential memory reminded him that he had once actually visited the house. He had been ten years old. On Saturday morning he had been dressed in his best, his newly trimmed hair brushed until his head ached, and driven in a hired car to the house with his father.

Mr George Rainby, it was explained to him, was an important county gentleman. The invitation to visit him was a rare privilege. Furthermore, he was a bachelor, unused to small boys, so Martin must sit still, not sprawl, and on no account speak unless he was addressed. Tucked under his father's arm had been his most prized stamp album: the reason for the summons. There had been a mention in the local paper of Mervyn Ellis's hobby and photographs of several of his rare stamps. It appeared that Mr Rainby was also a philatelist and had expressed a desire to see the stamps.

Mr Rainby, tall, cadaverous, slant-eyed, had regarded Martin with alarm, as though he were a savage animal who might go berserk. A manservant had served his father—sickeningly obsequious—and Mr Rainby with Madeira, handed Martin a glass of orangeade. After he'd taken a few sips Mr Rainby had coughed nervously, suggested Martin might like to take his drink into the garden. Hearing the neighing of a horse, he had found his way into the stable yard where he had been lowering a bucket into a well that was still there when he was chased off by a groom. At that point a shutter slammed down on memory.

The crumbling house with its high slate roof provided a focal point while his senses recalled Sheila's compliant body against his—acceptance yet, in the end, rejection. A woman with a fortune, who could not conceivably be in love with a toad-husband! She prated of goodness but to him that was a totally meaningless quality. It had never got anyone anywhere. That she revered it—if she did—was beyond his comprehension. More likely, with or without Desmond's compliance, she used it as a protective cover for her marital infidelities. That she was available to any man who struck a response in her, sent a surge of hot anger through him, bringing to mind the striking, nonchalant figure who'd stayed only long enough to announce he couldn't stay. Peter. A rival? He beat off the creeping unease. The woman who had lain with him on the bed of heather was, unless his powers of deduction were on the blink, wholly committed to no man.

Wealth and Sheila, his whole future transfigured! One half of his brain was unable to digest the immensity of his good fortune; while the other was racing towards the goal, feasting on the rewards. For once a genuine solemnity invaded him. It was an opportunity unlikely to occur twice in a lifetime. If he wasted it, it was lost forever. So every move he made must be perfectly executed. Every second spent in her company must be engineered to bring him nearer to victory.

For a second he felt exhausted, as though he'd been put through a grinder. With a backward glance at the cottage, checking that the door was still closed, he swung his legs over the wall, stared sightlessly at the empty house. Minutes later a movement alerted his attention. Two women were walking through the thigh-high grass of the orchard towards a gate that would lead them out on to the steep grass slope where sheep grazed.

When he heard the dog bark, he stood up, leaped back over the wall. A man standing in the open doorway whistled and the dog loped back to the cottage.

He was waiting for her halfway down the path. When she saw him she came running, propelled forward by the steep descent. He caught her in his arms, held her breathless body against his. He could have her, he thought exultantly; it was merely a matter of tailoring the when and how to please her. To ensure that at the end of an hour's pleasure, he had shifted her allegiance from the boring do-gooder Desmond to himself.

He held her hand, swung it, as they walked to the car. "What do you do with yourself in the evening when Desmond is about his good deeds?"

"I'm learning to play bridge."

He wondered if she were joking, but her expression showed no sign of it. "Why bridge?"

She said seriously: "I'm busy catching up on the education I never had. I've a long way to go yet. Anyway, most nights Desmond is home in time for the nine o'clock news, and in for an hour or so after school."

"Lunch? Thursday any good?"

"I've a date with a girl friend, but I might be able to duck out of it. Give me a ring on Thursday morning."

And with that, sensing that to press her harder would bring him no advantage, he had to be satisfied.

Miss Pilkington was a well-preserved spinster of sixty-two, autocratic and aggressive by nature. The demise of her ninety-year-old father, resulting in the theft of her ancestral home by a nephew to whom the estate was entailed, involved her in the purchase of a house. After the initial shock, she found it a challenge to which she responded with zest. There was no call for haste. Peregrine wouldn't throw her out—he hadn't the guts.

Of the three houses on her short list, Quarry Vale came at the top, partly because it was in such a deplorable condition that any sane owner would rejoice to be rid of it, so that, even in these days of inflated property values, she could count on a bargain. Secondly, it offered her unlimited scope for conversion. This was her third visit, and she intended to make a number more before she embarked on the highly enjoyable game of beating the price down to the figure she was prepared to pay. On her second Elaine Lowther had been detailed to act as the agent's representative. She had not chattered, airily dismissed as of no serious consequence dry rot, faulty damp courses and cascading tiles, and Miss Pilkington had stipulated to Robson & Bates that Miss Lowther should be present on all future inspections of the house.

Dressed in rain-resistant thorn tweed, wielding a man's stick, her intention today was to concentrate on the outbuildings, garden, orchard, and also the sheep-grazing leased to a local farmer.

Elaine, by now familiar with the client's intrepid nature, was dressed to explore cobwebbed attics, or find herself dropping through rotting floorboards, followed at Miss Pilkington's heels, as she hammered supporting timbers, rapped the disintegrating cover of the well, elated by the evidence of rampant decay. She emitted a snorting chuckle every time she pried a sagging gutter from a wall.

The garden, Miss Pilkington declared, would have to be ploughed up and replanted. The same went for the orchard: rotting and diseased trees, nothing to do but uproot and bonfire them.

She strode towards the gate that led to the pasture. Elaine, conscious of the heat on her back, wondered how Miss Pilkington could bear the heavyweight suiting, the woollen stockings. When she saw the figure of the man on the skyline, seemingly staring down at them, she stopped dead in her tracks. The sheer blast of astonishment, a suspicion that she had built an apparition in her mind, frightened her. But it wasn't so. Her long sight was exceptionally good. The oculist joked: "You'd be worth your weight in gold in a crow's nest, Miss Lowther." It *was* Martin, who had now disappeared from view.

Five minutes later Miss Pilkington chided: "What's the matter with you? Lost your breath? A young gel like you should be able to run up a little hill like this. I asked you who lives in that cottage?"

"Billy Corbett. He's blind. There's just him and his dog."

"Who owns the cottage?"

"He does. The previous owner allowed the tenant, who was Billy's father, to buy it, though not the land."

Miss Pilkington snorted, stumped off to the boundary wall and glared over it. "Thereby depreciating the value of the property. A cottage that overlooks the house, over which the owner has no control! No privacy! I find that a very invidious situation."

"Miss Pilkington, Billy is blind. He lives alone."

"He has sighted visitors." She pointed with her stick. "Getting into that car in the lane."

Martin and a girl with red hair whom he kissed before he went round to the driver's seat.

EIGHT

On Wednesday evening, when Elaine reached home, Martin was in the final stages of clearing out the garage. His aim was not only to get the car under cover, but for it to cease to be a marker as to whether he was in or out. Smoke from a bonfire in the back garden surfaced above the chimney pots; a pile of deck chairs and collapsible garden furniture was strewn across the lawn.

While he'd heaved and thrown out, his mind had been weaving in and out of labyrinthian calculations. With a fortune winking at him on the horizon there still remained an interim period to be negotiated. Sheila was bright enough to have a precise idea of her own worth—had probably fought off a dozen men who'd been after that unique package deal of beauty and wealth. Any whiff of evidence that his financial state was other than sound, and she'd turn suspicious, become too wary to handle. But once he was half owner of the hotel it should be comparatively simple to edge her towards making a modest investment in its modernisation.

However many times he retotalled the figures, adding to the miserable remnant of his inheritance the silver, ring, stamps, and furniture, he was still in dire need of Elaine's thousand pounds to nail Folk down, cajole him into having the deed drawn up. To be safe he should have the notes in his hand when he returned to London. Suddenly the tightness of the time sequences involved in handling Sheila, Elaine and Folk simultaneously made him feel like a high-wirewalker in a gale.

He stood and watched Elaine lock her garage door, gambling that the sight of him would act as a magnet and draw her across the road. The gamble paid off. Loathing the sight of her, a smile of welcome required a hugh effort, but he managed it. "Hi! Forgive the mess and muck. I've burnt a mountain of rubbish and there is as much again for the dustmen to collect."

She congratulated him and asked how he was fixed for supper.

"I went into town, had a steak lunch and bought a cold pie. I also collected a bottle of Scotch. If you don't mind hanging on while I wash the dirt off, come and have a drink."

She waited for him in the sitting room. Drawers and cupboards had been emptied, the contents piled on tables and chairs and, when the horizontal surfaces ran out, on the floor. All of which proved, when driven to it, he was both industrious and methodical.

There was no sign of the stamp albums or the gun. When he came through the door, she asked him what he'd done with the revolver.

"I shall hand it over to the police," he said, dismissing a subject that was none of her business. "Say when!"

As she lifted her glass of Scotch, he remarked: "The valuer came this morning, and a Mr Cheetham from your outfit looked in this afternoon to take particulars of the house to put it on the market."

"Yes, Graham told me he was coming. I hope you make a quick sale."

"You can say that again. I can't afford to be away from the Eglantine too long." He sat down, tried to conjure up a subject that would jerk her memory about the money, without sounding overanxious to get his hands on it—and failed. Since they couldn't drink in silence, or if they did his nerves began to shake, he asked: "What's your job at Robson & Bates now?"

"I'm Kenneth Robson's assistant. Mostly I deal with prospective buyers, show them over properties."

"Interesting, I should imagine," he murmured dutifully.

"Provided you can hold on to your patience and stamina. I was at Quarry Vale House yesterday afternoon with Miss Pilkington, a hard-bitten old spinster who's been dispossessed of her home by a nephew to whom it is entailed. My guess is that she'll eventually buy Quarry Vale, but at the moment she's enjoying herself too much keeping everyone on tenterhooks to admit it's what she wants. It's in a deplorable state of neglect because the previous owner died without leaving a will and all his relations have been fighting one another for nearly two years. Part of the thrill for Miss Pilkington is getting a bargain."

He remembered the two women climbing. If she'd looked up, she could not have failed to see him. Was that why she'd been at pains to prattle on about the old spinster? To serve him notice of her spying? He felt a choking sensation in his lungs, a wild rage that the pattern of his childhood and youth was, even now, being repeated: what he believed was secret was never so from her. He gulped the rest of his Scotch which gave him an excuse to turn his back on her while he helped himself to a refill. When he looked round, her cool, inscrutable gaze was pinned on him.

"Have you decided about the money? Whether you are prepared to accept it?"

That she'd finally broached the subject subdued his rage, lit a flame of hope. "It's all so damned tricky."

"In what way?"

Inspiration failing him, he resorted to a half-truth. "By the time I'm likely to get it, probably months hence, I won't need it. But right now, I have to admit it would come in handy. You see, I'm in the process of buying a half share of the hotel I manage. The owner is old, crippled, about to retire to the country, but he doesn't want to sell out his entire interest. I've finally nailed him down to letting me buy half. It's . . . well, quite an opportunity. I want to grab

83

it. But the old boy's a hard bargainer. There's still a gap between his asking price and the money I can raise. A thousand pounds would bridge it. What I'm saying is that by the time the estate is settled up and you receive the thousand pounds from Redditch the deal with Folk—that's his name—will be finalised one way or the other."

"What you're saying is that you want the thousand pounds now?"

"It sounds ungracious, damned rude but, yes, that's what it boils down to."

Her mouth was a fold of irony. "You imagine I keep a thousand pounds in my current bank account!"

"You'd be a fool if you did. I've already explained I've reservations about accepting Dad's legacy to you. In fact, I'm definitely against it. But since you offered it to me, what I would be prepared to accept would be a thousand pounds purely as a short-term loan that I'd repay with interest as soon as Dad's estate is settled. If you want a definite date, we could make it January 1st."

He hardly dared to look at her face but when he did so he found it bore no affront. Her eyes between the waxy lids didn't even look startled, only deeply considering. "That's an entirely different proposition, isn't it? I'll have to think about it, see if I can work something out."

He longed to scream: "Don't bother," but he couldn't afford the luxury. "Whatever you decide I'll always appreciate the gesture you made. It was extremely generous."

"No it wasn't," she contradicted quietly. "It stemmed from a guilty conscience. Last winter I suggested your father install a night bell that would ring in my bedroom. He didn't take to the idea, but I know he would have agreed if I'd pressed him harder. I didn't."

"No blame attaches to you. It's morbid to imagine it does." He gave a sigh of impatience. "The police still haven't caught the murderer. Since they picked up the silver on Monday, I'd say they'd been dragging their heels."

She made no comment, but got up, thanked him for the

84

drink, said good night and, when she reached the door, turned back to repeat: "I'll think about it."

Inside her own home, she climbed the stairs, kicked off her shoes and lay on the bed, her eyes closed. He was as insatiably greedy for money as he'd ever been. Parts of the pattern were falling into place, but the picture was a long way from complete.

At eight o'clock when he'd wedged the Rover in the garage, eaten a cold pie and a lump of cheese, Martin decided it was high time he telephoned Folk. Around eight-thirty Beckley, who in London doubled as nurse and occasional receptionist, usually went out to have a drink at the pub on the corner, leaving his master watching television, the internal telephone at his hand.

For a long interval there was no answer, and when it came it was from Beckley, as breathless as if he'd run up six flights of stairs.

"Mr Ellis here. Let me speak to the boss."

"You can't. He's in hospital."

"What?"

"A stroke on Sunday morning. He didn't regain consciousness until yesterday." Beckley's voice was hoarse with dry sobs or some other emotion.

As Martin, appalled, listened to the sorry tale, there surfaced in his head the visages of Sebastian Folk's sole remaining kin: his great-nephew Bernard and his wife Daphne. Bernard's mean, shrewd as a shady lawyer's, forever trying on dead men's shoes for size, and Daphne's fat and good-natured to the point of vacuity. If Folk died, they'd get the lot, and the deal would be off.

Beckley's voice, restored to its normal creeping tone, was sounding in his ear ". . . terrible shock, but Mrs Grimshaw and I are managing and all the guests are being very co-operative."

Martin cut in: "Which hospital is he in?"

85

"St Margaret's. Mr Bernard had him moved into a private ward, insisted he should have every comfort money can buy."

"I'll be down." Martin rang off without saying when.

Elaine woke to the sound of a car firing. It was 5 A.M., not light, but the room filled with an opaque pearly greyness. It could have been any car from half a dozen houses up and down the road, but her instant reaction was to check. She watched the Rover being backed to the curb and turned in the direction of town. At 5 A.M. were you likely to set out on a short journey? Hardly. Martin must be embarking on a longer one, probably to London. Her hand dropped the curtain her fingers had gripped. With the red-haired girl as his companion? It seemed a reasonable guess, but short of following him she'd no means of confirming it. What she didn't have to speculate was whether he'd come back. He'd do so to collect the £1,000 he believed she was prepared to give him.

Before he entered the hospital Martin rang Sheila from a call box, explained why their lunch—if she'd been able to fix it—was off. She sounded casual and uncaring. She wouldn't have been able to meet him anyway. He had to press hard to persuade her to give him another date. Saturday, maybe, but he'd better ring her in the morning to make sure. Desmond was taking a group of boys on a rock-climb. She'd see. For ten miles he fretted at her elusiveness, the streak of caprice in her that threatened to lay waste his hopes, but as the London end approached, he needed all his concentration to cope with the situation awaiting him.

When he entered the narrow oblong that was Private Ward No. 3, two hunched, muttering figures by the bed made an ugly blot on the cream and white décor. Bernard wore a funereal dark suit, Daphne was in navy blue, dabbing her eyes with a screw of a none too clean handkerchief.

At the sight of Martin, Bernard's whey-pale elongated visage assumed an expression of extreme belligerence. With a glance at the heap on the bed that showed no sign of life, he hissed: "How dare you barge in here? What are the staff thinking of! I shall complain to the consultant. Get out this instant."

Daphne sniffed, tugged imploringly at his arm, whispered: "Not here, dear, please. Go outside and talk."

In the corridor, Martin asked: "Well, how is he?"

"In a critical condition, not to be disturbed, or seen by anyone except his family. How you could have the affrontery! I shall take immediate steps to ensure you are barred from entering his room."

"He's my boss. I have my rights."

"Not with my blessing." Bernard breathed hard through his stuffed-up nose. "You cheat and bamboozle him for your own ends. A ship's steward engaged to manage an hotel!" He snorted wrath and contempt. "Now clear out and don't show your face here again."

Since Bernard was undoubtedly registered with the hospital authorities as the old man's next of kin, Martin had no ground for argument, or room to manoeuvre. He sauntered off. If you arrived by car there was only one exit from the hospital. The grim Victorian building was faced by a row of small shops, among which was a cheap café. Martin had to spin out coffee and a snack for an hour before, huddled together like two small-time conspirators, Bernard and Daphne emerged, climbed into their ancient car, and backed ineptly out of the hospital courtyard.

He made his way to the third floor. This time there was an engaged card on the door. He waited, fidgeting and staring at the NO SMOKING sign. A nurse, young, thank God, opened it. "Sorry, no more visitors until three."

He aped pitiable distress. "I've driven nearly three hundred miles to see him. I only heard the news last night. It was a ghastly shock. I still can't get over it. Couldn't you give me five minutes?"

"Sorry, no. He's asleep now. His nephew and his wife have been sitting with him for two hours, and now he must rest."

"Oh, God!" He put his hand dramatically over his face to hide his unmanly emotion. "I only want to see the old boy, just for a minute. Maybe for the last time. You see, after my parents died, he brought me up, gave me all I've got. Then, a year ago, we had a row and I walked out."

"How wretched for you. I am sorry."

"Five minutes," he pleaded. "Just sitting by his bed without breathing a word. You can stay and keep an eye on me if you like."

She shook her head, but with a hint of indecision. "If anyone found out, I'd be for the hatchet. Dr Mainwaring is due any minute."

"If he comes, I'll swear I just opened the door and walked in without asking anyone's permission. Please, it means the world to me."

"If you promise you won't touch him, speak to him, and you can only stay two minutes."

"Promise. Promise. God, you don't know what it means to me. Just to look at him, that's all I want, while he's still alive."

Sebastian Folk's skin was a hideous shade of yellowish-grey. The bags under his eyes were dyed purple. His arms stretched down his sides were as lifeless as an effigy's, and his hands cold and puffy. Martin beat a tattoo on one of them: rap, rap, rap, with two fingers.

Folk opened one eye, blinked it in slow motion several times before he managed to focus it on the figure by the bed. "Martin," Martin said in a voice raised as high as he dare—the old man was deaf. "Come down to see how you are and what do I find? Gone and got yourself into hospital! How are you feeling?"

The mouth slid into a one-sided leer. The voice uttered

88

a string of gibberish. Then the one eye closed and the face again resembled that of a corpse.

Martin stumbled to his feet. Outside the door he had to gulp hard to fight down nausea and fright.

The nurse coming back, said kindly: "I should go down to the canteen on the ground floor and buy yourself a cup of tea."

"He isn't going to make it, is he?"

"Now, now," she admonished cheeringly, "that's no way to talk. I've seen worse cases than his that have walked out of here on their own two feet—not that there's any hope of him doing that as he's a paraplegic. But it's amazing what excellent recoveries some stroke patients make."

He was still gulping air. "He can only open one eye and when he talks . . ."

"His speech may improve gradually, and he had two eyes open earlier. Dr Mainwaring is a marvellous consultant. He fights for his patients to the last breath. So don't give up hope." She smiled at him, then hedged her bet: "Of course, Mr Folk is over seventy! Still, come back and see what he's like in another week."

He thanked her, and because his knees felt weak took the lift down to the ground floor. A week. She meant that in a week Folk would either be dead or on the road to recovery. He knew enough about strokes to take into account a third possibility: Sebastian Folk might be no more than a hulk of flesh, without a working brain or a voice box that could frame words intelligible to the human ear. If he recovered, would Folk, frightened by a brush with death, be more amenable to terms? Could he spin him a tale about his father's extensive property taking a while to realise, and meanwhile hand him £1,000 in notes as a sweetener? There was no definite answer. The only certainty was that if Folk died or remained a mindless creature, Bernard would throw him out on his ear, and he'd have nothing but his modest savings and Elaine's thousand pounds—if he got that—until months hence, when Redditch handed him the pitiful dregs of his inheritance. And Sheila! In his distracted mind, her image became smaller and smaller, until it vanished.

With an effort, he pulled himself back to the here and now. His first task was to get to the Eglantine, reassert his authority, make sure it hadn't been usurped by Bernard's stooge, Mrs Grimshaw.

He timed his arrival for two when, lunch over, he'd catch Beckley and Mrs Grimshaw indulging in a protracted coffee session in the office.

But first he had to ease his way through a clutch of elderly residents who, apart from meal times, seemed permanently to roost in the fast-disintegrating wicker chairs in the entrance hall. They clung to his arm, cooed and clucked, were pitifully apprehensive about the future of the hotel as it affected them and were by turns optimistic and ghoulishly pessimistic about dear Mr Folk's chances of recovery. Martin had long ago made himself an expert in a soothing conciliatory manner that was utterly meaningless whether applied to a leaking tap or the probable demise of the proprietor. By the time he disengaged himself three of them, including one of the two male guests, were in tears.

Mrs Grimshaw, the housekeeper, second in authority to himself, had near-purple hair, what her grandfather would have termed a fine figure, and at fifty-odd wore her skirts above her knees to show off her plump but shapely legs. Sprawled in his swivel chair behind the desk in the midget office, she nodded but did not speak. Beckley, shrivelled in appearance, timid and devious by nature, seated in an upright chair, failed to rise but said civilly enough: "Good afternoon, sir. This is a sad occasion, especially coming on top of your own trouble."

Martin looked at Mrs Grimshaw. "If you could get me a cup of coffee."

Her automatic reaction to any request was to refuse it. "We're shorthanded, as you well know, and the kitchen staff are washing up." They engaged in a battle of wills it was vital Martin should win. In the end she dragged herself up. "I'll see what I can do. But I don't promise anything."

When she'd disappeared, Martin said bracingly to Beckley: "I've just left the hospital after seeing Mr Folk. He's making headway."

Beckley looked genuinely baffled. "That's not what Mr Bernard said. And poor Mrs Folk was so upset last night I had to get her a drop of brandy."

"I had a word with the doctor and his view is that within a week we'll see a great change for the better."

"Praise be," Beckley said and added, though he'd never said a prayer in his life, "then our prayers will have been answered."

"Meanwhile, I'd like to have a look at the books."

Beckley stared at his bony knuckles, muttered: "Mr Bernard's been seeing them twice a day when he comes in to give us the latest bulletin on Mr Folk, and to take care of any matters that need seeing to."

"Very obliging of him. But, as manager, while Mr Folk is indisposed, the books and bookings are my responsibility."

Beckley, who was incapable of standing up for himself in a direct confrontation, meekly produced the books. Martin scrutinised the cash receipts, the outgoings and advance bookings. Bernard had already signed this week's wages cheque, which suggested he must have been at pains speedily to acquire a power of attorney. To protect his interests, he should not budge from the hotel. But to safeguard another—Sheila—he couldn't afford not to.

Mrs Grimshaw entered with a luke-warm cup of coffee, a good proportion of which she'd spilled in the saucer. Her slate-hard eyes summed him up—signalling she had a shrewd idea of his dilemma and was relishing it. "I haven't seen any mention in the papers of the police picking up the man who murdered your father."

"They haven't caught him yet."

"So we shan't be seeing you back for a while yet?"

"I shouldn't take that for granted. I shall spend the rest

of the day here, and all Sunday. And I'll be back for good by the middle of next week. Meanwhile, I'll telephone you night and morning."

She said with sly malice: "With you so busy with your private affairs, there's no need for you to put yourself out. Mr Bernard's here twice a day. With Mr Folk lying like a log, he counts it his duty to handle all his uncle's affairs."

"Always provided Mr Folk wishes him to do so."

"He's not likely to be able to tell us that, is he! And as his sole relative, Mr Bernard has his rights. Even you can't dispute them."

Much good it would have done him if he had. He inspected every room in the hotel, had a comforting cliché for each guest who accosted him, ate his evening meal in the dining room, lodged complaints about the cleanliness of the table linen and the interval between clearing the soup plates and serving the entrée. Having ascertained from one of the residents that Mr Bernard usually paid his evening visit about 8:30 P.M. he left the Eglantine at 8:15. Until it was known whether Folk was going to live or die, nothing would be accomplished by brawling with Bernard.

Mrs Grimshaw having needled him into committing himself to a definite date of return to duty, he was under a compulsion to draw up a timetable, so tight that it scared him. By Tuesday night, Wednesday at the latest, he had to prise that thousand pounds out of Elaine. Also establish a link with Sheila that she could not—more important would not wish to—shrug off. His mind moved, with hope, in the direction of a hotel halfway between London and Coldbridge. No, not halfway, say an hour's drive from Coldbridge, which would leave him the major distance to cover. In theory he had one full day off a week, plus one half-day, but it had suited him only to take them when it pleased Folk —which was rarely. Now, with Sheila at stake, that one free day a week became the lynch pin of his future.

Elaine was in bed, the curtains open, no light in the room but a faint silvering of moonlight, when she heard the car

92

stop. It was 1 A.M. With the headlights on she could observe him opening the garage doors, getting back into the car. He nearly missed his footing, and moved as slowly and ponderously as though he was mildly drunk or totally exhausted. But exhausted by what?

NINE

Anthony James Ramsgate was arrested sleeping rough on the North Bay at Scarborough early on Friday morning. Shortly after 10 A.M. he was hustled into Coldbridge Police Headquarters with a blanket thrown over his head, the significance of which wasn't wasted on those who witnessed his arrival.

Superintendent Drummond sanctioned Naylor's request that, as he had dealt with the previous charge and knew the boy, he should conduct the first interrogation.

Tony, only recently emerged from shock, stuttered: "How come I had to be half suffocated?"

"Did you want to have your face in every newspaper in the country? Turn out your pockets."

They yielded 36p., half a bar of milk chocolate, and a penknife. The rucksack contained a pair of jeans, a spare set of underwear and six paperback books, two of them on Buddhism.

"First, how did you come by the pair of solid silver candlesticks and the silver cigarette box you sold to the firm of Amos Branding in Mossway, Manchester?"

"I haven't a clue what you're talking about."

Since Herbert Tilson, Amos Branding's assistant, was in the process of being brought by car from Manchester to identify the seller of the stolen property, Naylor didn't waste any effort on disproving a lie that would be done for him in under an hour. "Movements since you left home a week ago last Sunday. In detail."

There followed a capsulated account of his stay with Auntie Maggie, the effort to find work, and when it wasn't forthcoming, the hitchhike to Scarborough, the failure to find a job there.

"Suppose we get down to a few hard facts," Naylor suggested. "On Saturday, the 9th, some time after 7:30 you stole a cream Ford Cortina from the driveway at 10, Crossways Road, the property of Mrs Katharine Knight, and returned it during the night. Meanwhile you drove it around and parked it at the top of Fenny's Slope." In the interests of justice Naylor lied. "There are fingerprints on it that don't belong to the owner or any recent passenger."

Tony stoically deliberated. The habit of lying to his mother protected her from sickening bouts of distress, and to save himself from their nerve-racking effects was now so endemic it was impossible to break. But if, for all his careful wiping, they had found his fingerprints on the car, lying would only sink him deeper into trouble.

"I borrowed it," he said stonily. "For two and a half hours. I took it back safe and sound, parked it where I found it."

"Stole it. To take a bird for a drive, then parked it for whatever games you were up to, to keep you warm and dry. Remember it rained all evening and half the night. Who was the bird?"

For the first time in his life Tony knew the precise position of his heart; for a second it stopped dead in his breast, and then began to beat like a sledgehammer. "There was no bird."

"We've a witness. You and a girl were parked in Mrs Knight's Cortina on the verge of Fenny's Slope between 10 and 10:30 P.M. on Saturday the 9th September. I repeat: you and a girl. What's her name?"

"I never parked anywhere near Fenny's Slope. I just took a ride around alone."

"You're lying, and it won't do you a happworth of good." As a slip of paper was handed in to him, Naylor got up. "The shop assistant to whom you sold the silver had a good

96

look at you. He remembers that ring you're wearing, and he's got a false signature on the receipt form. George Blake! Fancied yourself as a big-time spy, did you?"

Receiving no reply, he temporarily abandoned Tony, said to the constable: "Get him a cup of tea. May clear his head."

Herbert Tilson had no difficulty in picking out the youth who'd sold him the silver from the others lined up in the identity parade.

"So there we are," Naylor said, when he, the constable, and Tony were back in his office. "You stole Mrs Knight's car, took a bird for a ride and a bit of snogging. After you'd taken the bird home, returned the car, your shortest route back to your mother's flat was to cut across Fenny's Slope. On the way, you saw a light burning in No. 8, Hartfield Road. You broke in through the French window at the back, slugged Mervyn Ellis to death, and stole three pieces of silver which you took to Manchester and sold to Amos Branding."

Tony was temporarily beyond fear. "You're saying I battered an old man to death! Man, you're real crazy."

"Well, prove it. Start by telling me how you came to be in possession of the three pieces of silver. Found it, maybe, chucked in a ditch."

"It was lying in the grass. I fell over it."

"Where in the grass?"

"On the common. I can show you where."

"I bet you can. There are four acres of common and you can pick any place that takes your fancy. You're not very bright, are you, lad? Okay, so what have we got, you stole a car, picked up out of the grass three valuable articles of silver which didn't belong to you, which you sold. Two criminal offences. That'll do for a start. We'll have a statement from you now, and then maybe by tomorrow, when you've had time to come to your senses, we'll have another. Later this afternoon you'll take part in another identity parade. We have a witness who saw you in the Cortina with a girl.

So try real hard to remember the girl's name and address."

There was a ten-minute interval with a policeman guarding the door, before an officer entered to take down his statement. Because Tony's mind in moments of extreme stress sought relief in indulging in bouts of fantasy, he thought of a rack. He saw his body subjected to excruciating pain, heard himself groaning aloud, yet in the end he emerged triumphant in that they had not prised Juliet's name from his lips. He bowed his head and prayed to a god in whom he didn't believe to be granted strength, and when the door opened the officer coming to take his statement was set back on his heels by the tears pouring down the youth's face. He seemed an easy touch and yet, according to Naylor, he hadn't broken.

At the end of a divisional conference, Drummond summed up: "He admits finding the silver, selling it and stealing a car." His glance fastened on Naylor. "Have forensic finished examining his clothes?"

"Not the ones he was wearing when he was arrested. All clothing at his home had been washed by his mother, every stitch he possesses. Shoes and sandals polished, even the soles."

"Does your wife polish the soles of your shoes?"

"No, but she isn't a demon for cleanliness. Elsie Ramsgate is. Since she was deserted by her husband when Tony was six months old, she's worked herself halfway to death to keep them both decent."

"And, naturally, would lie her head off to protect him!"

"Naturally. All right, he admits stealing the car, and it's conceivable that he did find the silver somewhere, though I'm not suggesting he did. What I am saying is that we're not home and dry until we've nabbed the girl, and so far we haven't got an admission out of him that he was with one, let alone her name.

"When are Miss Harris and her boy friend due?"

"Six. It's all laid on."

Mary Harris was a member of the Methodist Church, a strong-willed young woman ruled by her conscience, and not amenable to suggestion or coercion. Arriving at Headquarters escorted by her fiancé, she immediately said what was uppermost in her mind. "If you've only got the boy, Inspector, I won't be able to help you. It was the girl I saw. As our headlights flashed over the back of their car, she turned her head. I saw her face quite distinctly and could pick it out in a crowd. But the boy, or it might have been a man for all I know, he never as much as looked round. All I saw was the back of his head."

The fiancé, of different moral fibre, was acutely embarrassed at finding himself in a police station, being questioned about the exact timing of a highly private interlude. He swore, with truth, that if he'd noticed the car, he'd been unaware of its make, colour, or how many people were in it, let alone their sex.

The police were insistent. Mary Harris was made to walk down the line. The lips of a boy with a thin haggard face and fear shadowing his eyes trembled as she examined him, and she guessed he was the one the police wanted her to touch. But it was the first time she'd ever seen his face, so how could she?

Rosie, who'd been asked by the police to walk down the same line of male statues, was equally unable to identify the man she'd seen running across the road through a windscreen view distorted by a streaming torrent of rain.

"It's no good. I'm sorry. It might help if you threw a bucket of water over each of them. You see, wet hair is a different colour from dry. But I'm sure I couldn't identify him anyway: one moment he was there and the next he'd vanished."

Half running from the police station she collided with Robert. Though the *Argus* had gone to press with a bare statement that a youth was helping the police with their enquiries, and any further news would be of no use to him until tomorrow's edition, he had stuck around. Drummond had announced he would be giving a conference at 7 P.M. and then, later, cancelled it. He wanted to sniff out why.

Rosie, so sick of the whole business she was shaking, moaned: "I was only doing a good turn. There's this old woman Mummy goes to see once a fortnight. I promised I'd take her place while she was in Canada. I went latish, well, it was the only time I could go with that week's duty roster, and I thought she'd be about ready for bed. Not a bit of it; apparently she's some sort of night owl. She would insist on making tea and forcing me to eat a piece of horrible caraway-seed cake that I can't stand."

"Hold on, love! If Bruce were here, he'd give you a stiff drink. Since he isn't, I'll do the job for him."

A third of it drunk, she wailed: "You know what I wish, that I'd kept my mouth shut. There were kids in that identity parade or whatever they call it, some of them not out of their teens. And the police are going to charge one of them with murder."

Robert who had a normal reporter's access to classified information answered: "They've got a youth of nineteen picked up in Scarborough, who sold Mr Ellis's silver at a shop in Mossway, Manchester. He stole a car for an evening's joy-riding, returned it later to the driveway from which he lifted it. It so happens that the quickest route from there to his home was to cut back across Fenny's Slope, which means he'd pass along the rear of the houses in Hartfield Road. All highly suspect, but they're nowhere near clapping a murder charge on him yet."

She swore: "I'll never read another detective novel. It's so beastly when it happens under your nose."

"It was pretty beastly for old Mr Ellis."

"I know." She looked on the verge of tears. "I don't mean to sound callous. And it's beastly for Elaine. After it happened she was in a state of shock for two days. And then, well a bit crazed. Anyway right off-balance. Will she have to give evidence at the trial?"

"Since she found him, yes."

Later, as he walked her to her car, she squeezed his arm. "You're a pet, Robert. You've done me a power of good." She darted one of her most winning glances at him, dimples showing. "I wish you'd ask Elaine to marry you, and I wish she'd say yes. Why don't you?"

"Why don't you mind your own business?"

"Because I worry about her."

So did he, interminably, on many counts, but he wasn't prepared to admit as much to a pretty rattle-bag like Rosie. "That's no excuse for prying into my private life."

On Saturday morning Tony was brought before a special sitting of the magistrates' court, charged with the theft of a car, three pieces of sterling silver. At the request of the police he was remanded in custody until Monday week, and granted Legal Aid.

Elsie Ramsgate had the utmost difficulty in convincing herself that the proceedings she had witnessed had actually taken place. On leaving the Court, she demanded an interview with Inspector Naylor and, since he wished to see her, he agreed to her request.

She was dressed in her Sunday clothes, her calm almost traumatic, as she led with a stern but to her mind wholly justified rebuke. "It's a simple case of mistaken identity. Even you must realise that, Inspector. These days when all boys grow their hair long, wear jeans and anoraks, you can't tell them apart. That man from the shop in Manchester may not have deliberately told a lie, but it wasn't Tony who sold him the silver."

"Elsie, Tony has admitted both picking up the silver and selling it."

"Then he's shielding someone else."

"You're right. He is. A girl. He was seen with one in a car at the top of Fenny's Slope, but, presumably with the idea of protecting her, he won't admit it. So, Elsie, tell me about his girl friends."

"He hasn't any."

"Nineteen and no girl friends! Think again."

"Not for the last year, not since he was put on probation for touching a car handle! While he was at the Tec. there were one or two, but when he refused to go back, they dropped him or he dropped them."

"Tell me about the one or two."

"I don't know that I can. It's a good twelve months since I as much as saw him with a girl, or a boy either. Absolutely closed in on himself he's been since that night when you arrested him."

Naylor, not one to be distracted by a mother's wiles, insisted: "Try."

"There was one he brought home for a cup of coffee. I can't remember her name—maybe I never knew it. All beads and bangles and a fringe dripping over her nose, and long wavy hair, almost frizzy."

"What colour, the hair I mean?"

"Black."

"And the other?"

"She was a proper little podge, looked a sight in trousers, brown hair cut as short as a boy's, or as boys' used to be. And that's all. He never brought any others home."

"And you still insist you don't know what time he came home that Saturday night?"

She stared him out. "We used to have a row every time he came home and found me sitting up. When he was nineteen that's what he asked me for as a birthday present: that I'd promise not to wait up for him. He made such a set-to about it that I gave in. That night I'd gone to bed as usual between ten and half-past. He takes care to come in quietly so he'll not wake me. And he didn't." To make sure her face betrayed no shadow of guilt she blotted from mind that hour-long retching. Her memory was no more perfect than the next person's. She persuaded herself it had happened on a different night.

"And next morning, Sunday, he was off to Manchester to stay with his Auntie Maggie?"

"He often goes. He's been three times this year. Having two girls and no boy, she spoils him. Then she has more time and money than I have." She paused to get the better of her bitterness, said firmly: "I want to know what's going to happen to him now. I've a right to know. Being on remand, does that mean he'll be locked up in prison?"

"He'll be in a special wing of a prison, but not a prisoner. He'll have certain rights and privileges. You're entitled to see him, send him what he needs in the way of clothes, money to buy extras from the canteen. If he wishes he can have his meals sent in—but his diet shouldn't be all that bad."

"He's a faddy eater."

"Well, you can fix all that when you see him. A solicitor, Mr Charles Palfrey, has been appointed as his legal representative. He'll want to see you before Tony appears in Court on Monday week."

"And what then?"

"That depends upon the result of the enquiries we are making and how his solicitor advises him."

She drew herself a little higher in her chair, contemplated him with a terrible intensity in which there was no room for anger or resentment. In fact, she did not see him clearly —only as a symbolic, all-powerful representative of the Law, capable of laying-waste her son's life. She was looking deep into the soul of the child she had borne and raised, forcing herself, for his sake, to a decision that withered part of her. When she spoke it was calmly, factually. "There's something you should know about Tony. He tells lies. He always has when he thinks that the truth would hurt me or anyone else. His trouble is that he can't bear to cause pain, but there's not a streak of viciousness in his whole nature. Ask anyone who knows him, and they'll tell you the same. So if you're trying to make out he battered a poor, helpless old man to death and stole some odds and ends of silver, you're helping the real murderer to get away Scot free."

She rose to her feet, suddenly vested in dignity. "That's the truth, Inspector. God's truth. You talk to his Probation Officer, and he'll tell you the same. Tony's only weakness is not being able to stand the sight of anyone being hurt. In that way, I suppose you could say he's a coward, but he never lies to protect himself, only other people."

TEN

Martin anguished to himself: not a peep out of Elaine since Wednesday! If he was to have the cheque for a thousand pounds in his pocket before he left Coldbridge, he had no alternative but to make a move himself—insufferable though the idea was. As soon as the shops were open on Saturday morning, he drove into town and bought an impressive bunch of chrysanthemums.

When she opened the door, he ceremoniously presented them. "Rather belated thanks for a splendid Sunday lunch."

She thanked him, took them a little vaguely, as if she couldn't think what to do with them, and then stood back so that he could enter. "Have you had breakfast?"

"An hour ago, but I'd love a cup of coffee. That old percolator produces the vilest brew."

She made a pot, carried it into the sitting room, and silently poured cups for both of them.

He leaned forward, said with a throb of satisfaction: "I expect you've heard the police have caught Dad's murderer. He's to be charged this morning."

Elaine, who had talked to Robert on the telephone the previous evening, gave him a hard, probing glance. "But isn't he only to be charged with stealing and selling the silver?"

He waved the question away. "Hair-splitting! Whoever stole the silver murdered Dad. The police are merely tying up the evidence. They'll probably have completed the job by the time they produce him in court."

She appeared wholly engrossed in sipping her coffee. In a plain denim dress, her legs bare, her feet in sandals, no make-up, with her hair brushed to a shine and tied back with a blue ribbon, she looked younger; different in a way he couldn't positively define. Her silence, as though his arrival had interrupted a deep reverie from which she hadn't yet surfaced, unnerved him. Then everything about her kept him tense and uneasy, forever on the watch for duplicity.

He cleared his throat. "I've had a shock since I saw you on Wednesday. My boss had a stroke last Sunday. He's in hospital in London. I went to visit him on Thursday. After I'd seen him I had to go along to the hotel and check up on how things were there. With Folk sick in hospital, and no deputy, the situation's turned dicey. By rights I should be back there permanently."

"Couldn't you manage it, now that you've finished clearing out the house?"

Abandon Sheila? Leave Coldbridge without a clue as to whether or not Elaine intended to hand over the thousand quid? He felt his fist ball up with the desire to smash into the face that maddened him because it hoarded the power to keep him guessing until there would be no point in guessing any more. Unbalanced, simple-minded, or downright crafty, which the hell was she?

He shouted: "I want the satisfaction of seeing the brute who battered my father to death in the dock. Do you find that unnatural?"

"No." She put down her coffee cup. "But with the owner of the hotel seriously ill, won't it mean that your plans for buying half of it will have to be shelved for the time being?"

He felt a pinch of horror. She was going to duck out . . . now. He managed a firm, reasonably authoritative tone. "Not necessarily. Some patients make a fairly quick initial recovery from strokes, though there's a long haul before they are completely recovered. If that happens in Folk's case, I can see him beginning to fret to have the deal signed and sealed."

106

"But would his doctors, anyone concerned for him, permit him to discuss business at this stage?"

Only Bernard ably abetted by Daphne. Again he was inwardly thrown into a panic by the pressure of time linking hands with events to defeat him.

Deciding his ends would be best served by conceding her point, he swallowed his rage. "You may well be right. I'm going to see him tomorrow, and I'll know more then. The nursing staff at the hospital were fairly optimistic on Thursday, and the old boy has plenty of guts. He's looking forward to life in a country pub, and he'd be wild to have it snatched from him."

He waited, nerve ends twitching, for her to mention the thousand and when she didn't, drove himself to do so, tuning his voice to an offhand but conciliatory note. "About the loan, I don't want to rush you, but I wondered if you'd had time to consider it and come to a decision. A short-term loan with interest, that is."

"I have been thinking about it." She paused, fixing her tranquil unblinking gaze on his face, as though bent on tormenting him. "It would mean selling out some investments. When would you want it?"

"Frankly, as soon as you could manage it."

For a second the blandness of her glance was shot through by one so keen and piercing that his mouth dried with fright. She said incredulously: "You honestly believe your boss will be fit to talk business within a few days, to sign legal documents?"

"Could be," he said with bravado. "Money—or rather making it—is what keeps him alive."

She looked away from him, her eyes carefully out of his reach. "I'll try and make an appointment to see Mr Winston some time on Monday. He's my bank manager."

"I'll pay you whatever rate of interest he suggests."

"I'll tell him that," she said gravely. "Another cup of coffee?"

He hadn't been able to drink the whole of the first cup.

The old demoralising fear began to seep back. Powerless to read her quirky mind, he could only form wild speculations. Was she keeping him in suspense as a form of revenge? If she offered him the cheque, was she going to extort some form of payment for it other than interest? And, wilder still, could she conceivably know all about Folk and Bernard—and Sheila? Was she, in fact, what he'd believed her to be in his youth, a she-devil with a third eye, a carrier of doom into whose hands he had witlessly delivered himself?

When he'd gone, Elaine went upstairs and opened her jewel case which held the string of pearls her father had given her mother the day she'd been born, her mother's old-fashioned rings and pendants, and her own collection of amethysts and garnets. She lifted out the top tray, stared at the small cylindrical object she'd wrapped in tissue paper, not touching it, only making sure it was there. When she replaced the tray, closed the jewel box, she found the flesh on her arms so chill, she took a cardigan from a drawer and covered them.

Again, he left it to Sheila to choose the venue for lunch. She picked an hotel on the other side of Big Tor. The food, though below the standard of the shooting and fishing hotel, was reasonably good.

When they reached the coffee stage, Martin broke through her light, mildly amusing chatter to remark: "So Desmond's a rock-climbing enthusiast, is he?"

"As an exercise in character-building for the boys, yes. He set off at nine with fifteen members of Form V. Mountain rescue teams to be alerted if they've not reported back to the school before dusk."

"He's a glutton for punishment. If you were my wife, I'd be a strictly ten-to-five man. I wouldn't trust you, and how right I'd be!"

She teased good-humouredly: "Then, you're not a very trustworthy man yourself, are you!"

The question bounced out of his mouth: "Do you love him?"

"I respect him."

"For God's sake!" He grimaced revulsion. "A woman like you can't exist on respect. What's more, you don't."

"You may be right." Her voice was cool but firm. "Anyway, I'm not prepared to argue."

"You play games," he accused, "rather bitchy little games. Do you want me to drive you home?"

She shrugged. "If you want to. But not if you don't." Suddenly she gave him a narrowed, puzzled look. "You're the most impatient man I've ever known. You act as though the world was going to end tomorrow."

"You can't blame me. At least you wouldn't if you were sitting where I am, looking at you."

Mollified, she put a finger on his hand, then withdrew it. "So what's the answer? I don't fancy a prickly bank of heather, certainly not the back of a car, and my nearest neighbour is a widow who spends half her time at her window with a pair of binoculars focused on my front door."

"Then it's up to me, isn't it?"

"Yes. Any suggestions?"

Desperation, plus the need to establish some indissoluble claim on her that very afternoon, fired his brain, sent a succession of images shooting through it, out of which he seized one. "How good an actress are you?"

She raised her eyebrows. "What on earth do you mean? I've never attempted to find out."

He leaned forward, whispered: "Then try now. Give it all you've got. If you can come through with a good performance we should be home and dry. Sink your head in your hands, lean over the table. When I call the headwaiter over, moan and act as though you're about to pass out. And leave the talking to me."

His wife, Martin apologised to the alarmed headwaiter, was unwell. Probably because they had driven too long a distance for a woman in the first stages of pregnancy.

Brandy was brought. Sheila couldn't force it through her lips. She lay bonelessly, eyes closed, while Martin diffidently suggested that the only remedy was for her to lie flat for a couple of hours in a darkened room. Was there a vacant one they could take for the afternoon?

The housekeeper was summoned. There was a vacant bedroom on the second floor, but as there was no lift, wouldn't it be better for Madam to retire to a small lounge on the ground floor?

Martin pleaded the need for the remedial prone position, with the minimum of light. Assisted by two waiters and the housekeeper, Sheila's limp form, knees buckling, was conveyed upstairs. Within a couple of hours, he promised the beady-eyed housekeeper, who showed a disposition to linger, his wife would be sufficiently recovered for them to continue their journey. If it wouldn't be too much trouble, could they be served with a tray of tea at four o'clock?

When, with dragging feet and backward looks, she finally left them alone, they were so elated by their brilliant double-act that they had to stuff their fists into their mouths to stifle hysterical laughter.

In the dimness, from the bed, she stretched out her hands to him, cried in flattering surprise: "You're a whole lot smarter than I thought. On the spur of the moment you managed to work a small miracle."

"I'll work another," he promised, as he began to ease the clothes from her body, with its narrow hips, full breasts, and unflawed silken skin. Pride in his brilliant manoeuvre brought in its train a surge of confidence. He rode the clouds, was a king in his own right. Floating on the rim of his vision, reduced to meaningless trifles were his scheme to persuade Elaine to give him a thousand pounds and the running battle with Bernard. What the hell did either of them signify when matched against his mastery over Sheila! Mind and body were whirled in a stream of passion, and as it lost momentum it was replaced by sensations to which he was a stranger: peace and tenderness towards his partner. Love, he marvelled, damn it that's what it was, love! The genuine gold-plated article. For a few seconds he was humbled that desire and ambition had been handed him simultaneously.

"You know something," she said drowsily, "you're good, damned good."

He pressed her palm to his lips. "The best. Come on, admit it, you've never had a better lover."

Without warning she began to cry. The little hiccoughing sound dismayed him, ate a hole in his triumph. He held her bare flesh hard to his, kissed her mane of burning hair, tenderness overflowing. "Sweetie, it's going to be good for us for ever and always." To see into the depths of her eyes, he moved her head on the pillow. To his astonishment they were dry.

She complained: "It doesn't help that you manage an hotel in London and I live in Coldbridge. Which of us commutes?"

The lightning speed at which her mood could change from passionate dependence to shrewd practicality bruised his ego. "Trust me. I worked two miracles, and the third will come up the moment we need it." He checked his watch. "You've ten minutes to dress, sit up in that chair, looking frail and pregnant."

"It's just as well I never forget my pills."

He asked, suddenly curious: "Don't you and Desmond want any kids?"

"He does. I don't."

Jealousy pinched. "Why?"

"I'd want to give them everything, a perfect life." As she stooped to pick up her tights, in the dimness, her face took on a strange mystical look. "Secure and safe in a magic circle. That's how you feel about having kids if you had a childhood that was sheer hell."

"We'd be so happy we'd be the safest couple in the whole world. We'd have everything, plenty left over for half a dozen kids." He pulled her hard against him. "Well, wouldn't we?"

"Maybe." She eased herself free. "Maybe."

There being no second post on Saturday, from 9 A.M. Juliet was reduced to a state of abject despondency interspersed with flashes of panicky alarm. Her flesh and bones proclaimed she and Tony were one, their minds so perfectly attuned that their thoughts moved in unison. But on Monday, in the barn, there had been that odd little flaw in communication almost, on his part, a dodging behind a curtain, as though—the suspicion was ridiculous—there was deceit between them.

The afternoon she spent in her study-bedroom, supposedly sorting through her clothes to prepare a list of any items she needed for the Finishing School. In fact, she sat at her white desk, a transistor playing, fondling the letters and a receipt for cash received from the travel agent.

At four her mother entered with a tray of tea. She could have acted as a model for an idealised young matron. Her figure was trim but rounded, her grey-blonde hair softly styled, her moss-green jersey dress expertly tailored to show off her slender waist.

She gave her only child a loving, amused smile. "Honestly, sweetie, isn't it boring sitting and listening to pop music hour after hour?" Without waiting for an answer, she went on: "Decided what else you'd like for Fullwick? You're low on cocktail dresses. How about a new one; say one of those long patterned cottons you liked in that boutique off the High Street? And, please, one good fitting pair of slacks to make a change from your disreputable old jeans, eh?"

"I've plenty." Because her convent manners stuck, Juliet added: "But thanks, Mummy. If I find I'm short of anything, I can go into Cheltenham and buy it."

Her mother shrugged tolerantly. "I wish you'd go out more. It's been a perfect afternoon. You could have borrowed my Mini, gone visiting one of your girl friends." She scanned the desk, but the letters and receipt were back in the drawer, and the top clean except for a leather blotter and the transistor. "You know Daddy and I are going to the Mainwarings' party this evening? That's if he gets home. I shan't wait for him. If he's hung up too long he may decide to give the party a miss. Trudy Mainwaring understands, or she should do by now. Will you be in?"

"I expect so."

"There's a chicken casserole in the oven, ready any time between seven and half-past, and a coffee soufflé in the fridge. Now, darling, for heaven's sake don't let me come home and find all you've had for supper is an apple and a bite of cheese. You eat so little you worry me to death."

"I'm fine. With my size if I ate all you put before me, I'd be square. And I promise I'll see Daddy has a good meal if he's too late to go the Mainwarings'. Honest!"

Mother and daughter smiled at one another. Juliet was a precious only child, born prematurely to a woman who could bear no more children. The relationship between them was warm and solidly based, though on Juliet's side it largely consisted of habits that were a hangover from childhood. It often irritated her intensely that she felt bound to be courteous and considerate to her parents.

When her mother had left the house, Juliet wandered through the rooms and out into the garden, movement an easement for unease. The morning papers were laid in a tidy pile in the sitting room. She reached for the top one, then changed her mind. Except for running her eyes over the headlines she had ceased reading newspapers months ago. There seemed nothing in them relevant to her and Tony. The radio served her better, where her ears acted like a sieve, relaying to her only rare items that affected them.

Into the garden again. It was dusk, the trees her parents had planted when they bought the house before she was born, huge dark shapes against the fading sky, her father's gaudy begonias shadows of themselves. On the way into the house she picked the evening newspaper from the letter box.

The headline hit her like a blow: ELLIS MURDER. Anthony James Ramsgate charged with stealing three pieces of sterling silver from a house in Hartfield Road, and a car, the property of a Mrs Knight. Like a sleepwalker she carried it, still reading the print, into the sitting room. Tony had appeared before the magistrates' court that morning, and at the request of the police had been remanded in custody until Monday week, granted legal aid.

ELEVEN

Tony shared a two-bunk room with a boy of sixteen, arrested for pilfering cigarettes, who cried most of the night. In the evening, when they'd been in the open room watching television, Tony had seen a copy of the *Evening Argus* with his name spread across two columns on the front page. He was news: by implication not only a thief but the murderer of a crippled old man, a fact that was underlined by the glances that hung on him with horror, sly awe, or stark curiosity.

So, like everyone else in Coldbridge, Juliet would know. There entered his mind in slow procession the people who'd be prepared to swear the police had arrested the wrong man. He could count them on one hand. A master at school who'd taught him English and introduced him to Dylan Thomas. Jimmy Trouncer who'd been his buddy until, Heaven help him, he'd joined the Army. Cynthie, a gypsy-like girl he hadn't seen for a year and, oddly, coming up behind her, a girl whose name he couldn't even remember. She'd stood in as a temporary leader at a Youth Club he'd joined for a short period years ago. For some curious reason her face remained fixed in his memory: cool, but not with a cold coolness, more as though she were in total possession of herself; alternatively, maybe she didn't care sufficiently about any issue to lose her cool. Whichever it was, it had given her a serenity and a poise that had lodged fast in a remote corner of his mind. Then, isolated on a sort of throne was his mother: his cross as he was hers. Her face as he'd left the witness box forever stamped into his head in the shape of agony, shame, and iron-hard disbelief.

And Juliet, his love, the journey to an earthly paradise reduced to a dream never to be fulfilled, to be protected, not from hurt, not from grief, that was impossible, but from involvement. At all costs. He lay in his bunk, his hands locked behind his head, neither hearing nor heeding the snivelling boy, in a trance of composition of a behaviour pattern that would save Juliet from herself.

At two o'clock on Sunday afternoon Juliet, having asked directions from a policeman in Market Street, drove her mother's Mini into the parking space of the prison on the southern outskirts of Coldbridge. The Remand Centre was sited in a brand-new wing at the rear. She gave her name to an officer, was directed to the visitors' room, where there were a dozen small tables set out in a double row, each allotted two chairs. About half of them were already filled. A warder produced a slip, filled in the name of whom she wished to see, and waited while she signed it.

It was ten minutes before he returned, by which time enough visitors had arrived to create a continuous buzz of chatter. "I'm sorry, miss," he said, not sounding in the least so, "but Ramsgate insists he doesn't know you."

"Of course he knows me. You must . . ." Her voice stopped abruptly. So that was how he intended to play it! She tore a page from her diary, wrote on it: *Nobody's going to get me out of this dump until you show up. I'll do a sit-in for a week if I have to.* She handed it to the warder, ordered rather than asked him to deliver it to Tony.

The page crumpled into a ball in his palm, he stepped into the room as though he expected it to be booby-trapped, wary as a hunted animal. He stood poker-stiff on the other side of the plastic-topped table, and when she touched his hand, snatched it away. "Buzz off. I don't know you. I've never seen you in my life."

She said with muted savagery: "Don't forget I can see

into your head. You should be able to see into mine. You can if you try hard enough."

The next couple, a girl talking to her father, stared at them so fixedly that Juliet dropped her voice to a whisper. "Forget it, will you. This kooky idea you've dreamed up is a non-starter. I can blow it up in your face any time I want. And I will."

He looked at her with eyes as dead as a sleepwalker's, his mouth opening just sufficient to emit the dreary little chant: "I don't know you. I've never seen you before."

That he could look at her so, as though she were his mortal enemy, brushed her spine with chilling horror. For a second, while she gathered her will to renounce what her eyes had seen, she closed her lids. When she opened them, she could laugh. "Sir Galahad, riding on a white charger! My, what a fall you're heading for."

He repeated like a litany: "I don't know you. I've never seen you before in my life. Go away and stop pestering me."

She gazed at him with the impatience with which she'd have regarded a fractious child. "Okay, I'll go away, but only to prove exactly how well you know me." She angled her head, smiled her serenest smile. "You stole the silver to pay for your ticket to Katmandu, and you borrowed a car to keep us dry in the rain. So, big deal! They can send you to prison for a few months, which means we'll have to wait for Katmandu until you get out. What's the odds! You murdering a crippled old man!" She giggled to emphasise the absurdity of it. "You couldn't squash a beetle! I know you. Remember, we're not two, but one."

Elsie, who'd reached the prison by taking three separate buses with long waits in between, tapped her son on the shoulder. Juliet, who knew who she was without looking at her, tossed off: "No goodbyes, Tony. Be seeing you."

Elsie stared fixedly after the tiny, high-stepping figure, demanded in alarm: "Tony, who was that? She talked as if there was something between you? Is there? What's her name?"

"I don't know her, and I don't even know her name. She came to see some other fellow and struck up a conversation with me."

Elsie savoured the lie. It was an old pain but still savage. "You'd better know right away that the police are interested in your girl friends. Sergeant Naylor's been asking me for their names."

He shot a look at her jumping with suspicion. "What did you say?"

"That I didn't know any names. How could I! You never bring any home."

"I haven't got any to name." He eyed her with a burden of responsibility that bred hate. "You shouldn't have come. It's a dead loss. I don't suppose you got a lift, did you?"

"You know very well I'm not one for cadging lifts."

When Juliet got home, she took Saturday's *Evening Argus* out of her desk. The solicitor appointed to defend Anthony James Ramsgate was Charles Palfrey, a golfing friend of her father's. She considered telephoning him at home, then decided against it. Too risky. His first move might well be to contact her father. Better to be waiting in his office at 9 A.M. tomorrow morning.

Sitting opposite to her in the bar of The Three Kings, Robert reflected with satisfaction that for the first time he'd not had to coax Elaine to have a drink with him. The date had actually been her suggestion. Without inviting her to choose what she'd have he ordered champagne cocktails.

She gave him a glance of happy surprise. "What's the celebration? We must be celebrating something."

"In a way you could say so. I've finally made up my mind to go back to Fleet Street."

Halfway to her mouth she set her glass down, then quickly raised it again. "To you. If you're happy, I'm happy for you. Coldbridge was only a temporary halt, wasn't it?"

"When I came I wasn't sure. But I suspect you're right.

There's been a shakeup of the management, and I'll have a new editor."

She raised her glass for the second time. "Here's to all you want."

He nearly said: "That means you." Instead he asked lightly: "Any chance you'll miss me?"

"Every chance." Her smile was warm, for once without qualification. "Coldbridge will never be the same again and the *Argus* will be reduced to a shadow of itself."

"You flatter me! Let's drink up and have another round."

"No," she countered, "not until I've told you why I wanted to see you."

He aped dismay. "Not for the pleasure of my company!"

The weak joke bypassed her. "About four years ago I knew Tony Ramsgate. For three months, while one of the leaders was away on a course, I substituted for her at the Youth Club in City Road. Tony was a member; might still be for all I know."

"So?"

"I happen to remember him; I can't think why. Perhaps because he was a different type from the hoodlums and show-offs. In a negative way he was friendly and helpful. He'd volunteer for a dirty job, like sweeping out when the caretaker was off sick. Gentler, too, than the rest of the mob. One night a mongrel dog came in, and while all the others chased it round, he got hold of it, took it into the kitchen and gave it a drink of water and some food before he took it to the police station."

"He certainly seems to have made an impression on you."

"I admit it's odd since I've never given him a thought from that day to this. Perhaps because there were a lot of skinheads about in those days with girls as tough as themselves and Tony made a refreshing change. But that's not the crux of what I wanted to tell you." Her glance, direct and deep, found his, almost as though she were making a plea, the granting of which was immensely important to her. "He was frightened stiff by the sight of blood, his own or anyone else's. He'd practically keel over if he cut his finger opening a tin, and at the first sign of a brawl he'd quietly fade away. Yet, morally, I wouldn't have said he was a coward."

"Elaine, why are you telling me all this?"

She looked away, a cord in her throat moving, then she brought her glance back to his waiting one, said only just above her breath: "I found Mr Ellis." She paused, drove herself on. "One side of his head was beaten to pulp. His hands and arms were horribly cut. Before a quarter of the blood I saw had been spilt the Tony Ramsgate I knew would have passed out or bolted for his life."

"Four years! A boy when you knew him, nineteen now."

"I've taken account of the time gap, but I still can't see Tony Ramsgate, at any age, committing brutal bloody murder."

"He's not been charged with murder, only with theft."

"But there could be a murder charge, couldn't there?"

"Could be. At the moment there's a missing link. A girl. The police have a witness who saw her with him in a stolen car at the top of Fenny's Slope, though Ramsgate, while admitting he stole the car, swears blind he was alone. The police are pulling out every stop to trace the girl, but so far without results."

She leaned forward. "Should I go to the police about Tony? Or wouldn't they take any notice of what I say? Does it make sense to you? Do you think they'd listen to me?"

"They'd listen, but if they pile up sufficient evidence against him, I doubt if any statement of yours would have much effect at this stage. Your best bet would be to see his solictor, Charles Palfrey, give him what amounts to a character reference."

She looked unsure. "Would you hear in advance if the police were going to charge him with murder?"

"Probably, though it's not certain." He regarded her with puzzlement. "Why all this tremendous concern? A charge isn't a conviction."

120

For a second the glass partition that he imagined divided them, seemed to dissolve and it was as if love had breathed upon them and words would flow from her mouth that would free her from whatever bondage held her. Then she blinked suddenly, and the shadow of remoteness was back, as she looked down at her hands as if she'd never seen them before. "To be charged with murder at nineteen, even if the jury acquits you, would be pretty soul-destroying."

However sound her motive, he knew it would have no effect on any action the police decided upon. Instead of saying so, he repeated his suggestion. "Talk to Palfrey first." When she nodded agreement, he asked: "Is Martin Ellis still around?"

"Yes, but not for much longer. The owner of the hotel he manages has had a stroke and he's needed in London."

He asked because if he didn't she wouldn't be likely to tell him: "Do you see much of him?"

"Occasionally we meet coming in or out."

On Sunday morning, having left Coldbridge at 5 A.M., Martin spent two hours at the hotel endeavouring with all the force at his command to reassert his authority over the upstairs and kitchen staff. With the exception of one new, slightly subnormal chambermaid, they all smartly answered him back with "Mr Bernard" says this or that. It was Beckley's day off, but Mrs Grimshaw took a spiteful pleasure in ostentatiously making no comments on his orders, appearing not to allow her ears to absorb them. When he notified her that he'd be back on duty on Thursday morning, she retorted smartly: "Maybe you'd better let Mr Bernard know, see what he says about that."

At the hospital Bernard's car was parked askew, half-blocking an exit. Martin waited in the steamy, burnt-fat smelling café until, huddled deep in their coats, Bernard and Daphne emerged.

A bell was ringing when he reached the second floor. The

same nurse met him in the corridor. "Oh, it's you again! You're out of luck. That's the bell for the end of visiting hours."

"In a private room!"

"I'm afraid it makes no odds because Mr Folk's nephew has given strict orders that you're not to be admitted." Her uptilted nose gave a little twitch at the notion of intrigue. "Are you up to something fishy? After the old man's money by any chance?"

"If you were helpless on a bed, whom would you prefer to see, Bernard Folk looking like an undertaker arrived to measure you for a coffin or me?" He disemburdened himself of a box of chocolates with which he'd prudently armed himself. "Did *he* bring the old chap any roses?"

"No. But then a lot of men don't care for flowers."

"He does. He can't wait to retire to the country and sit in a garden."

All the while he'd been talking he had surreptitiously edged towards the door. "Ten minutes. You can stand on guard outside and time me."

"I've better things to do, but I shall come back in ten minutes and boot you out. I'm only going easy on you because Sister's caught up in an emergency."

"Bless you!" He dropped a whisper of a kiss on her cheek. She made a feint of slapping him. "That will get you precisely nowhere."

He grinned, paused with his hand on the door handle. "How is he?"

"Better than when you saw him on Thursday. His voice is stronger but it's still not possible to make out what he's saying. But pretend you can. If you don't he gets upset and that's bad for him. And there's some movement in his left hand."

"How long will he be in here?"

"That's for Dr Mainwaring to decide. My guess is that it will be a week or two before they even put him in his wheelchair."

Folk looked no different from Thursday. His skin was the same hideous yellowy-grey, and one side of his down-drawn mouth twitched in sleep.

Martin laid the roses between the old man's hands, touched the straighter of the two sides of his face. A Cyclops eye regarded him.

"It's me, Martin, come to see how you're getting along."

A flow of gibberish came through his lips and then tears gushed from the open and closed eyes and dripped down his chin.

At once nauseated, seized-up with alarm at the now or never effort that must now be made to get the simpleton in the bed under his control, Martin gulped down the bile. "Okay, okay. So you can't talk properly yet. But you can hear me, can't you? Just nod your head."

Fractionally, Folk, with a huge effort, managed to do so.

"Then there's nothing to worry about. I'll do your thinking for you. That's what you pay me for, isn't it? To be your think box. And I've never let you down, have I? Come on, another little nod."

Folk nodded, a firmer movement this time, the top layer of the pitiful scum of confusion lifting from his eyes.

"There you are, see. Everything under control." Martin brought himself to bend his head level with the old man's ear. "Now you listen to me. I'm back at the hotel seeing that everything is being done exactly according to your orders. No need for you to bother your head about a thing. But there will be if you let Bernard take over the place, act as though he owns it, which is what he's after. Oh, I know you're fond of Daphne. She's a good niece and a nice woman, but Bernard now, he's altogether different. Ambitious, greedy. I wouldn't put it past him to take advantage of your being in hospital to take over the place lock, stock, and barrel. And that wouldn't suit you, would it?"

Folk stuttered in terror. The monosyllable was almost certainly a no rather than a yes.

Martin's tone became more cajoling, though still retaining its ring of authority. "Now you and me, we think along the same lines. Your interests are mine. I've proved that, haven't I? And don't forget we're going to be partners. You taking it easy down in the country, me reporting to you every weekend, and the profit equally divided between us. With me you'll always be the boss. With Bernard you'd be the underdog."

He picked up the roses, brushed the old man's trembling chin with the red petals. "Come next summer, if you listen to me, you'll be sitting surrounded by your own rose trees, with me looking after your half of the Eglantine as well as my own. But give Bernard control, and I can't answer for the consequences. Why? Because I won't be there. I couldn't work for a man I didn't respect, and if I left most of the staff would walk out with me. To replace them, you'd have to pay higher salaries, and there'd be your profit running down the drain, not to mention the fat Bernard would skim off."

Tears of utter desolation dripped into the hollows in Folk's cheeks, lodged there, the misshapen mouth shaking as though he'd been smitten with ague.

Martin's relief that he'd hammered into the senile old fool the crucial point that, with Bernard in command of the Eglantine, he'd lose money, gave him strength to bend his face to within two inches of the hateful palsied mask.

"Now, I'm going to let you into a secret. I've got someone lined up who's prepared to invest money in modernising the hotel. A personal friend. More bathrooms, showers, a general face-lift, and we'll be pulling in the better-class tourist trade. Doesn't that cheer you up? By this time next year you'll be making more money from half an hotel than you are from the whole one now." He wagged an admonishing finger in front of the stricken face. "That is, as long as you don't put Bernard in control, which would mean I wouldn't be there to protect your interests. Come on, another little nod to show you trust me."

It came, the frantic effort at movement releasing another gush of tears.

On his way home, Martin told himself, though the afternoon had sickened and exhausted him, he'd done a good job on Folk, put a spoke in Bernard's machinations to gain control of the Eglantine that would, with luck, tide him over until Thursday.

TWELVE

Charles Palfrey's secretary, a beady-eyed spinster in her midforties, gave Juliet a skimming glance of disapproval and said tartly he was not likely to arrive at his office until 9:30 and, as he was due in court at ten, it would be impossible for Juliet to see him. She must make an appointment.

Juliet airily declined, sat in the anteroom, small feet tucked closely together, delicate hands folded in her lap, haughtily determined not to be deflected from her purpose.

At 9:40 Charles Palfrey greeted her with a cold look but a feigned hearty voice. "My dear child, Monday morning! If there's any advice you need, it'll have to be short and sweet, or wait until after lunch."

He offered his hand, but she did not waste time on shaking it. "It will take precisely five minutes."

He waved her ahead of him into his office. With half a generation gap between them he knew Juliet mainly through her parents. In any case the skinny fey-type was not for him. His wife was a cuddly, vivacious brunette. "Well, come on, let's have it." He checked his watch. "Ten minutes dead."

"You're defending Anthony Ramsgate, aren't you?"

"Yes." His interest, which had suspected a minor peccadillo such as a traffic offence, flared. "Yes, indeed."

"We're friends. You'd say we should be married, but that's not our scene. Yesterday afternoon I went to visit him at the Remand Centre, and he swore his silly head off he'd never seen me before."

Charles Palfrey, having a reputation for maintaining his cool under the most abrasive circumstances, strove to keep it now. "Who's right?"

"I've already told you. I am. He's putting on a big act to protect me. But I've proof that he's lying." She reached in her shoulder bag, held out a receipt for two tickets that would take the bearers from South London to Katmandu and a letter confirming that the tickets would be posted ten days before the departure date.

Charles's face that was plump-cheeked, with round eyes under bushy brows, looked like a startled owl. "Good grief! Do your parents know?"

"No."

Though it had suited him to state his presence was required in court at ten; in fact, his first case was not likely to come up before 11 o'clock. He pressed a button, snapped a request into a microphone that he was not to be disturbed.

His natural pomposity back in place, he assumed his suave professional mien. "If I'm to help you, you'd better give me the complete story, right from the beginning."

"There isn't a story beyond what I've already told you. Tony and I have been lovers for six months. In twelve days' time we're travelling to Katmandu by bus because that's the way we want it—and anyway, it's cheaper. From there on we'll play it by ear. We may return to England; or we may never set foot in it again."

"And you say your parents don't know of your plans?"

"They don't know." Full stop. "But I'm seventeen and there's not a thing they can do about it."

"You're a callous little devil, aren't you! However, that is beside the point. Ramsgate certainly won't be setting out for Katmandu and all points East in ten days' time. You know what he's being charged with?"

She gave a brisk nod. "That's why I'm here. The receipt and the letter, plus other letters I've got at home from the travel agent, prove that we planned this trip together. That's your job, to make him see that this crazy idea he's cooked up to protect me won't work. Anyway, once or twice we've been seen together. If necessary, I could produce a couple of witnesses."

When he did not comment but concentrated on marshalling his thoughts into a proper legal framework, she insisted: "I'll spell it out to you. On the night old Mr Ellis was murdered, Tony and I were together, in a car because it was pouring with rain. We parked on the verge at the top of Fenny's Slope. We were there from eight to—I'm not sure—but around ten, maybe later. Then he drove me home and . . ."

"And," he finished for her, "returned the car he'd stolen to its owner's drive."

"Yes." The elfin face did not reveal a flicker of discomfort, let alone guilt. "After that he went home himself, straight home. If you're thinking that he murdered a crippled old man, you're wasting your valuable professional skill and a lot of your very expensive time. He isn't capable of it."

He gave her what he counted as his most intimidating glare. "You'd better get a few basic facts straight. My job is to defend my client, not lay extra charges against him. He has already admitted stealing a car from Mrs Knight of Crossways Road and to being in possession of silver knowing it to be stolen and selling it. Two charges that do not include one of murder. He will appear before the magistrates a week today."

"I know that," she retorted witheringly. "But you'll be seeing him, won't you?"

"Yes. In all probability tomorrow."

"Then drum it into him that this crazy idea he's dreamed up of never having seen me in his life, won't work. Explain about the tickets—they'll probably arrive tomorrow with our names on them, and I'll wave them in the magistrate's face. I'm going to see him, talk to him, and no one, not even Tony, is going to stop me."

"I'll put your point to him. He's entitled, of course, to exercise his own judgment. If he maintains his present attitude, that's his right. Meanwhile, what do you propose to do about your parents?"

"That's my business."

"Not wholly. Your mother and mine serve on various committees together. I belong to the same golf club as your father. Later th' week mutual friends are giving a party at which I'll undoubtedly meet your parents. I'd be failing in my duty to them if I didn't point out to you most forcefully that they have a right to be informed of your relationship with a young man who is a self-confessed thief."

"I'll get around to it."

"I advise you to do so without delay."

She didn't give him the satisfaction of an answer. "And telephone me tomorrow when you've seen Tony. Why do you have to wait until tomorrow? Why can't you see him today?"

"Because, my dear child, I happen to have other clients in addition to Tony Ramsgate."

The Warden of the Remand Centre telephoned Naylor at home on Sunday evening. When he'd said what he had to say, he added: "I thought I ought to put you wise before I send in an official report and the slip with her signature." When no comment was forthcoming, he asked: "Stan, are you there?"

"Yes," Naylor replied, finding his voice. "You're dead certain, Ted? Couldn't be another girl of the same name?"

"No, unmistakably her. Quite a bit of her old man in her. Nice manners but rides a high horse and takes it for granted she'll get what she wants. Sorry, Stan. You'll have the report and the signature first thing in the morning. So, passed to you, eh?"

Passed to him to pass to whom! "Thanks, Ted," was all he found to say.

The telephone conversation flew into his head as soon as

he came to consciousness on Monday morning. It didn't necessarily follow that she was the girl in the car at the top of Fenny's Slope. She might, for all he knew, be dedicated to social and welfare work—her mother certainly was—and give them their due, quite a few kids these days were concerned with the aged, the imprisoned and the underprivileged. Again, despite Elsie's statement, Tony might well run a string of girls of whom the Sunday afternoon visitor was only one. In this age what was any mother permitted to know about the sex life of her daughter, much less her son!

When Naylor put in a request to see Drummond he was closeted with the Chief Constable. Leaving a message that he was to be called instantly he was free, Naylor killed time in the Operations Room. Though there was plenty of activity, the controlled frenzy that had operated until Ramsgate's arrest, was absent. To occupy the waiting time he borrowed the Log Book from Detective Constable Ralston—although he knew every entry by heart.

After ten minutes or so, Ralston remarked chattily: "Did you know we're running another check on Martin Ellis? Either he's got a shocking memory, or he's been lying in his teeth. Local police are making a closer investigation for us. It seems there's this old geezer in one of the hotels where Ellis . . ."

As a constable intimated that Superintendent Drummond was free to see him, Naylor replaced the Log Book under Ralston's nose. The drift of what he'd said had percolated Naylor's ears, but made no impact. Ralston was a keen and conscientious detective but, in Naylor's estimation, lacked the essential quality of being able to evaluate the weight and relevance of facts. Also he was overanxious to demonstrate that he knew more than the man he was talking to.

Stepping into Drummond's room, he doubted whether he'd ever have to face up to a more painful five minutes. To make it worse Drummond was in an unusually relaxed mood, his smile had a touch of genuine warmth, his air was less rigidly martial. Waving a well-manicured hand to a chair facing his desk, he enquired: "Well, what can I do for you, Stan?"

There was no conceivable gentle lead-in. It had to be played straight: factually presented, devoid of emotion. "Last evening the Warden of the Remand Centre telephoned me. You remember, we asked him to keep a record of any woman or girl who visited Tony Ramsgate. He had two visitors yesterday afternoon. His mother and a girl."

"Good!" Drummond nodded satisfaction. "It was on the cards the girl might turn up. Who was she?"

Naylor noticing the sweat marks on the slip he'd been grasping, laid it on Drummond's desk. "She gave her name as Juliet Drummond." He wanted to say: "Sorry, sir" but had enough sense not to.

Drummond's light blue gaze did not shift from Naylor. He had sufficient control over his facial muscles—and pride —not to permit the shock to which he'd been subjected to show. His voice when he spoke was clipped but untroubled. "Another of Ramsgate's inventive whimsies! He chooses to call himself George Blake when he sells stolen silver; tells his girl friend when she visits him to give my daughter's name!" His throat made a sound between a cough and a derisive laugh. While Naylor stared blind-eyed at the slip which Drummond did not acknowledge was on his desk, he challenged: "Well, isn't that your reaction?"

"Could well be, sir. But I thought you should be informed immediately."

"Of course. Thanks." He paused before he tossed off his next question. "Did anyone at the Remand Centre record a description of her?"

"Yes, sir. Young, seventeen or eighteen. Blonde, with long hair almost to her waist. Slightly built. Well-spoken."

A brick-dust seemed to rise slowly out of Drummond's neck and cover his face. His right hand moved across the desk to retrieve the slip, then he sharply drew it back. "Thanks. Obviously the first step is to prove that Ramsgate's visitor was not my daughter. It shouldn't take long. Then we can get ahead with the real job of tracing the girl."

Meryl Drummond could not remember an occasion when her husband had arrived home at 11 A.M. on a weekday morning.

With no brush of his cheek against hers, which was his habitual greeting when he left or returned to the house, he demanded: "Where's Juliet?"

"Why? Darling, what's wrong? She's in her room. She got in five minutes ago. I asked her if she wanted coffee but she said no. Frank, what is the matter? For Heaven's sake if it's anything involving Juliet, tell me. Don't frighten me to death. Frank . . ."

He edged her aside, said stonily: "I'd prefer to speak to her first. It may well be a stupid hoax. Most likely it is. If so, I don't even wish to discuss it with you at this stage." He went towards the stairs and on reaching the landing for the first time since she'd been a small girl, opened his daughter's bedroom door without knocking.

Inside the room he leant against it, as though his six-foot athletic frame needed its support, and watched his daughter turn in slow motion from her desk.

His voice when it came from his throat surprised him by its low pleading note—that of a man beseeching a favour. "Juliet, a report has been made to me which I believe to be untrue. I have been given a slip of paper which is said to bear your signature though it amounts to no more than a scrawl. All I want from you is a straight yes or no to the question I'm going to put to you. Did you visit Anthony Ramsgate in the Remand Centre at Silverton Prison yesterday afternoon?"

"Yes."

The inconceivable had happened. His reaction terrified him. He wanted to seize his fairy child, shake her until she screamed for mercy. Instead, he resorted to the classic formula for quelling temper: six slow, deep breaths. Then, though his voice had a harsh edge, it was not raised. "You admit to being the friend of a common thief; visiting him in the Remand Centre yesterday afternoon?"

"Daddy, please!" She gave a sigh of forbearance. "Don't you see, it's pointless your acting the outraged parent, as though I'd deliberately set out to betray you. It's happened. And now it has, there's nothing I can do about it, or want to, for your sake or anyone else's. And you can't blame me for not telling you sooner about Tony. He's a dropout from the Tec. He's no job, no means of supporting himself, much less me. And to your generation that's a sin, isn't it? You can't or won't understand it doesn't matter to ours. We're lovers, Daddy. That means we only want one another; nothing else matters."

He drew so hard on his breath he felt a pain in his chest and wondered momentarily if he was going to have a coronary.

Her father's expression, the strain under which he was labouring, both enraged and frightened Juliet. Pity, she'd renounced. It was a trap. Duty, too. But her nature that was not as callous as she'd led Palfrey to believe, found it more painful than she'd anticipated to discard as of no account the years of her childhood and adolescence. She closed her speedwell blue eyes, whispered: "Daddy, please try to understand. I know it's hard, but please try. I'm not your little girl any longer. I'm a woman. Tony's woman." When he made no response she opened her lids. He was just staring at her, but with such an unrecognisable expression in his eyes, that fear jumped alive in her, and she blurted out: "You'd have been hurt, anyway, even if this hadn't happened. I never intended to arrive at that silly Finishing School. Instead Tony and I were going to Nepal. We still are, when all this stupid fuss is over. That's why he sold the silver he found, to pay for his bus ticket to Katmandu because he's too proud to let me buy it for him."

Katmandu! A dot on the map below the Himalayas, awash with hippies doped to the eyeballs! Her abysmal defencelessness so appalled him that he shouted at her: "He also stole a car to take a girl for a ride. Were you that girl?"

"Yes, of course I was. Who else! He borrowed a car for a few hours to keep us dry because it was pouring with rain. He returned it to the drive from which he borrowed it."

"Stole is the correct word. We have a witness who saw you in that car with him at the top of Fenny's Slope. This afternoon you will take part in an identity parade."

"Why bother?" She sounded genuinely puzzled. "I've admitted being with Tony. Why should I deny it?"

"You might decide to, in court. You will remain in your room until three o'clock this afternoon, when your mother will drive you to Police Headquarters. There the procedure will be explained to you by one of my officers. When it is over your mother will bring you home. As soon as I can contact him, you will make a detailed statement to my solicitor, Tom Hardcliffe, of your association with Ramsgate, any part you played in the offences with which he has been charged."

She protested in a high childish voice: "You're acting like a policeman not my father."

"I happen to be both." They exchanged appalled looks at the power each wielded over the other before he went on: "If you attempt to run away I shall have you followed and brought home."

"You can't. I'm seventeen. A free woman."

"Not when you are the confessed associate of a criminal, a witness for the Crown."

Disbelief burned slowly across her face. "You'd do that to me!"

"Not I. The processes of the Law which I'd be powerless to stop. One more thing." He found it necessary to moisten his lips. "*You've* admitted that no one but Ramsgate is of any concern to you." He paused. "If you can avoid it, don't spell that out to your mother."

Terrified, she was about to burst into tears, and distrusting his reaction, he left abruptly. His own, unshed since he was six years old, were heaving behind his eyeballs.

THIRTEEN

The hotel Martin picked out was ninety minutes' run from Coldbridge, along a side-turning a mile and a half from the motorway. Sheila's Lotus would probably do it in less. On Monday morning, after Desmond had left for school, he telephoned her and suggested they have lunch, not at the same hotel but one near, in order that he could familiarise her with its exact location.

Her total lack of enthusiasm for the idea filled him with dismay, an appalling sense of communication between them run amok and, with Saturday less than forty-eight hours behind them, a deadening bafflement. How could she react so negatively? Lunch, she announced offhandedly, was out. She had a date. Jealousy gnawed, reason suggesting if the date were with a girl friend, surely it could be postponed, or at least her name specified. Then, a man? A picture of the confidently smiling man at the Sunday-night party flashed through his head, plus the sound his ears had recorded of the precise degree of disappointment in her voice when she'd heard he'd only looked in to say he couldn't stay. The total blankness of his knowledge of her comings and goings while Desmond was incarcerated in school was like a running sore.

It required persistent coaxing before, as Desmond was engaged on a play-reading session and wouldn't be home until eight, she agreed to drive out to the neighbourhood of the hotel late in the afternoon.

Putting down the phone, he swallowed the unpalatable

truth that she was adept in all the subterfuges of a woman well-versed in deceit, for instance, telling him to meet her in a church car park a mile outside Coldbridge. She was on time, but instead of transferring to the Rover, she said she preferred to drive the Lotus, which reduced him to a passenger, a role which further deflated his ego.

She talked while she drove, but on matters of no concern to either of them; on a par with casual chat between acquaintances. His responses grew more and more monosyllabic until she took a slanting glance at him, which was what he'd been angling for. "What's wrong? You're as grouchy as an old bear."

"And you're not!"

"Should I be, when you've been at pains to provide us with a love nest?"

The arch voice grated. He snapped back: "You haven't told me in so many words you'll join me there, have you? Will you?"

"I'm not sure." On an instant she turned serious, reflective. "Probably I will, provided the deal is foolproof. Do you remember I warned you about getting the wrong idea?"

"Such as?"

"Taking it for granted that Desmond would divorce me if I slept with you a hundred times. He wouldn't. I told you that on our first date."

"You certainly did." He believed, because he could not bear to contemplate any other alternative, that this was a situation she accepted because it suited her, but that, equally, it was a state of mind and body that fire and passion would render abhorrent. He said to gain precious time: "I'm not arguing. But that doesn't stop us from seeing each other. And, now I've found the hotel, all you have to do is to name the day—and night."

"All! You imagine it's that easy!"

A damn sight easier than it was for him to abandon the Eglantine to Bernard's conniving trickery for half a day and a night! "Don't you ever go to London to shop?"

"I spent three days there a fortnight ago on a buying spree for winter clothes. I can hardly take off on another."

Her refusal to indulge in subterfuge on his behalf both frightened and infuriated him, but he managed to ram both emotions out of sight. "Simple. You've had second thoughts about some dress or coat you bought, want to change it, or there's something you forgot to buy. I thought any woman could dream up an excuse for shopping if she wants to, and the urge is strong enough."

"It is." To his bounding relief she threw him the first sensual smile since they'd met in the car park. "Is that junction ahead where we turn off?"

"Yes. If you take the next left fork, there's a pub where we can have a drink. Afterwards we can circle round and I'll show you The Falcon." Without warning he had a sense of all the mountains he'd set himself to scale tumbling on top of him. He barely stifled a groan, then looked with unutterable longing at her profile. "Sheila, can't you understand, I love you." For the first time in his life he'd spoken out of the depths of his being, and she sat there as composed and untouched as if she were out for an afternoon drive with a friend. He shouted: "There, you've got it, spelled out. And it doesn't mean a damned thing to you, does it?"

She drove into a space where the hedge curved inwards, and when she'd switched off the ignition, she sat with her hands locked on the wheel looking straight ahead while she picked each word with deliberation to give it maximum weight. "That's not fair. I'm almost sure you love me, but I don't love you, not yet." She turned, her mouth grown tender, her eyes dark with thoughts he couldn't read. "But I do love you loving me. Truly."

That she could be so painfully explicit, subject love such as he'd never suffered before, to a clinical analysis swelled the doubts crowding in on him.

When he didn't speak but just stared at her, she pleaded: "Martin, I'm honest. At least grant me that."

"Yes," he said heavily. "But even honesty can't destroy

hope." For once, incapable of dissembling he clutched at the truth. "If you love someone, that's all you've got, hope."

She leaned forward, cupped his face between the palms of her hands and lightly kissed his mouth. When he tried to pull her to him, she resisted. "Hey! There's a car about to pass us." When it had gone, she said in a puzzled voice: "You're so ragingly impatient. No, worse than impatient, desperate somehow, as though, oh, I don't know, that you haven't a second to lose, that it's a now or never affair with you. Are you always in such a raging hurry over everything?"

That she'd been shrewd enough to sense the pressures of a timetable he couldn't control, alarmed him, but he managed a laugh. "Only over you. Every true love worth his salt is impatient." But other lovers had weeks, months, whereas he had only a fast dwindling sum of days.

They had three early drinks at the pub and then he drove her past The Falcon which was a medium-sized country hotel and club set in a small park. He pressed her hard for a firm date, and finally, after imposing a condition that she was free to ring him at the Eglantine and postpone the meeting if she couldn't make it, she agreed to a day a week ahead. They'd meet there in the late afternoon and stay overnight.

As though to seal the pact she offered to let him drive the Lotus back to Coldbridge. When they reached the church car park it was empty except for the Rover. In the dusk, behind a screen of enfolding yews, she made no protest when he took her in his arms. The taste of wantonness on her lips, a suppressed passion in her limbs restored his ego. Time, just a small piece of it would give him heaven on a plate. As soon as he got indoors he'd telephone and make the booking with The Falcon.

But when he reached Hartfield Road a car was parked outside No. 8. The Detective Inspector whose name he couldn't recall, who'd interviewed him on the day of his arrival, heaved himself out onto the pavement. As if the lapse of memory showed, he prompted: "Detective Inspector Naylor."

"Hello, Inspector. You're obviously waiting to see me. Come inside."

"If you've got five minutes."

In the sitting room Martin offered Naylor a drink, and when he refused poured one for himself, looking with distaste at the heavy, thick-skinned face with its hanging jowls, the old-fashioned slightly dusty navy suit with a frayed edge to one of the trouser turn-ups. Seedy was the word that sprang to mind.

Naylor brought his droopy bloodhound gaze up from floor level, fixed it on Martin. "Mr Ellis, in your statement you said that you were not aware of your father's murder until you returned to the Eglantine Hotel? Is that so?"

"Most certainly. That is why it was such a God-awful shock."

"Yet in an hotel at which you stayed in Launceston on the night of the 11th September, a fellow guest, Mr Francis Clavering, had a drink at the bar with you, and showed you an item in that day's *Daily Mail* which gave such details of your father's death as were known to the Press: his full name, address, that he was a retired bank manager, and the exceptionally brutal nature of his murder."

Martin looked at a loss. "You're mistaken, Inspector. Or rather Mr Whatever-his-name-is. I certainly stayed at the Kingsbourne Hotel for one night. I had a drink in the bar before dinner, and a nightcap before I went to bed. Naturally, I exchanged the usual pleasantries with the barman, other guests, but I can assure you that no one showed me a newspaper report about my father's murder. If he had, I'd have left immediately for Coldbridge. Why should this man allege he did?"

"Two reasons. Mr Clavering is over eighty. A year ago, being alarmed at the number of elderly people living alone who'd been attacked in their own homes, he decided to sell

141

his and move permanently into an hotel. Your father's murder lent support to the wisdom of his decision. He was, in fact, congratulating himself. Also he knew your name and was curious to find out if there was any relationship between you and the murdered man."

Martin laughed. "How many Ellises are there! You say he's old, over eighty?"

"Yes."

"Then there's your explanation. He imagined the whole thing, suffered the type of delusion common to old men approaching senility. Or, simpler still, showed the paragraph to some other guest whom afterwards he came to believe was me."

Naylor said equably: "Mr Clavering is not senile. Except for being somewhat deaf in one ear he is in possession of all his faculties."

"Deaf! Wouldn't that account for the discrepancy between his statement—it would seem he's made one—and mine?" His voice took on a harder, more indignant tone. "Inspector, if I'd known my father had been beaten to death, do you imagine I'd have continued with my holiday! It would have been against human nature. In any case, what possible reason could I have had in wishing to hide from you or anyone else the fact that I knew my father was dead?"

"That's what I wondered, Mr Ellis."

"One doesn't—couldn't—exist."

Naylor nodded, seeming to concede the point, reached for his shapeless hat and lunged to his feet.

"What I don't understand, Inspector, is why you considered it necessary to spend time and public money checking on my movements during the week I was on holiday."

"You made a statement, sir. It is normal police procedure to check all statements. Routine, Mr Ellis, routine."

Martin gave him a hard, penetrating glance, but the drooping lines, sagging and bagging, were such that they provided a loose-fitting mask for whatever thoughts were flowing through his brain. He demanded: "When are you going to charge Ramsgate with murder?"

"We're still proceeding with our enquiries, sir. You'll be kept informed of the outcome."

When Naylor disappeared into his car, Martin poured himself another drink, brooded over the lighted windows on the other side of the road, and over a third whisky braced himself to a decision. Time had run out for Elaine's devilish game of cat and mouse. Better to know the worst than to be trapped in a nightmare of suspense that kept his nerves jumping.

When the bell rang Elaine had just climbed out of the bath. She had few chance callers in the late evening, and though it could be someone with a charity collecting box, she knew, with that sixth sense that operated where he was concerned, that it was Martin. By the time she had put on pyjamas, a towelling robe, slippers, and combed her hair, he had rung a second time.

"Oh!" He sounded taken aback. "I didn't realise it was that late. Have I dragged you out of bed?"

"No. I've been climbing the roofs of Quarry Vale House with Miss Pilkington. I was so filthy I needed a bath before supper." She stood back to let him in. "Have you had yours?"

Her obsession with feeding him was a mounting irritation. "Yes," he lied. "But don't let me stop you."

"I'm in no hurry."

As he followed at her heels into the sitting room, he remarked for something to say: "Hasn't the old girl made her mind up yet?"

"My bet is that she has but she's enjoying herself far too much keeping everyone on tenterhooks to admit it. Now she's asked for a week's option on the property while she consults her nephew Peregrine. Actually she detests him because he's inherited her family home, so I doubt if she'll take his advice. It could be, of course, that she wants to make him feel guilty by showing him the tumble-down ruin into which he's forced her to move. Would you like a drink?"

"No thanks. I've just had one with Inspector Naylor. He looked in to check a minor point." He forced his lips into a smile. "I came over because I thought I should let you know I'll be leaving for London on Wednesday night or early Thursday morning. I would have preferred to wait until Ramsgate is charged with murder, but with my boss still in hospital, I have no option but to get back on duty at the hotel."

She gave him a sharp, searching stare. "Who told you Tony Ramsgate is to be charged with murder? Inspector Naylor?"

"Not in so many words."

She said slowly, mouthing every syllable: "Tony Ramsgate did not murder your father."

"Oh, come on," he jeered. "The case against him is about sewn up."

She repeated with the same hard emphasis as before: "He did not murder your father."

"How would you know?"

"I know him."

"Know Ramsgate?" He was startled. "How?"

"It doesn't matter." She repeated: "He's not capable of committing murder."

"Then how come he was in possession of the silver?"

"I didn't say he wasn't a thief."

He laughed, shrugging his shoulders. "You've lost me. Why are you so certain? And why are you so concerned about Ramsgate?"

"I'm concerned because I know him and I wouldn't like to see him sent to prison for ten or twelve years for a murder he didn't commit."

"Where's your faith in British justice? He'll get a fair trial."

"Even British justice isn't infallible. Men have been proved innocent of murder after they've been hanged."

"Capital punishment! It was abolished years ago. Ramsgate won't hang."

144

He began to wish he'd accepted her offer of a drink. At least it would have given him something to do with his hands. Rising in him was the old nemesis syndrome: that cold, clammy certainty that where he was concerned she possessed some quality akin to second sight. She'd drawn the curtains, and there was nowhere to look but at her, wrapped from neck to ankle in a baby-blue robe, matching kid slippers on her feet. It crossed his mind that she had deliberately set a seduction scene. His stomach heaved and heaved again, the urge to walk out, make sure he never cast eyes on her person again so strong it propelled him to his feet. Yet, somehow, he had to gather together every dissolving shred of will-power to make one last bid for the thousand pounds that was his only weapon against Bernard Folk.

"I wondered if you'd had any chance to get to the bank today?"

"I'm afraid not. I had to cancel my appointment when Miss Pilkington telephoned asking me to meet her at Quarry Vale this afternoon."

"What about tomorrow?"

She spent a long moment pondering to herself, then rose. "First, there's something I should like to show you."

He heard her climb the stairs, come down as slowly as though she were counting every step. In her hand was a thin, cylindrical object wrapped in tissue paper. She uncurled the twisted ends, laid it on the table beside his chair. He stared at it, baffled. "A ball-point pen! Why? I mean why do you have to show it to me? What am I supposed to say?"

"Whether or not it's yours. It's stamped with the initials M.E. If you buy a gross they'll print your initials on free. You see the advertisements in the small ads in the Saturday newspapers."

Not touching it, still looking bewildered, he asked: "Why produce it now, at this minute? If you're suggesting it's mine, you're mistaken. Having your initials stamped on a ten-penny ball-point is hardly my style. Anyway, where did it come from?"

"From the floor of the room in which your father was murdered."

"So why didn't the police pick it up?"

"Because I got in ahead of them."

"I don't get it," he said peevishly, "all this drama! Mervyn Ellis. Dad's initials. He must have treated himself to a batch."

"If he had, he'd have shown them to me, or I'd have seen him using one doing his crossword puzzle. Since he'd become housebound, except for small items he asked me to collect for him, he shopped by post. Partly because he hated to cause me trouble, but also because he enjoyed the excitement of parcels arriving. And part of the fun was showing me what he'd bought. In any case, it wasn't easy for him to strip off the sticky tape. I did it for him, or Mrs Selby did if she was on hand. I went to see her yesterday. She never opened a package of yellow ball-points stamped with the initials M.E. Neither did she see your father using one."

He shrugged. "I wouldn't know the answer—or see why anyone should care what it is. Probably left over from a batch he bought years ago. Hold on . . . it could be an old one of Mother's. Her name was Madeleine." He cloaked his detestation of her under a thin smile. "Don't you remember Dad used to call us the Three M's?"

She looked down at the pen, then raised her cool, unblinking gaze to his face that still kept the smile tacked in place. "I agree. It could have been your father's, even your mother's. It so happens that it isn't. It's yours."

"What the hell are you on about?" He glared fury at her. "And why are you making such an issue of a cheap ball-point pen?"

"I'll tell you, though you must have guessed already. Because you dropped it the night you killed your father."

He opened his mouth, closed it, then opened it again to bellow: "You're out of your mind, clean out. You're sug-

146

gesting . . ." He gazed at her with a rage of loathing, mouthed: "You're *that* crazy!"

"Crazy!" she repeated quietly, no whisper of emotion surfacing on her face. "Crazy to know, from knowing you, that you'd do anything, even commit murder to get your hands on your father's money if you were desperate enough for it. And you were, weren't you? To buy half an hotel. You had to have it instantly. I proved that by offering you a thousand pounds. All right, I admit it was a bait to test you out. One that worked." She gave him one of her cool, sealed looks. "You can still have the thousand pounds before you leave Coldbridge if you can prove to me that you didn't break into your father's bedroom and beat him to death . . ."

He reared up slowly out of the chair, stood before her, feet planted apart, the breath pumping in his lungs, hate a thunder in his head. "You're mad. A mad woman. A raving lunatic. You ought to be locked up." He saw his clenched fist shaking in her face, dropped it, calmed his voice to ice-cold venom. "Now I'll tell you my story. Why do you suppose I took off from Coldbridge? To get away from a dead-end job, a deadly home life? No. Because I couldn't stand another day of you dogging my heels, spying on me. The sight of you began to turn my stomach, make me want to throw up. But would you be shaken off like any normal girl! Not you, and you know why? Because you aren't one; you never have been. You're a freak, a goddammed freak!" He laughed raucously in her face. "Go on, run to the police with your ball-point. See what sort of reception you get from them. They've already got the man who murdered Dad. In case you've forgotten, his name's Ramsgate."

"I hadn't forgotten."

He went to the door, and when he reached it, turned and sneered over his shoulder. "And keep your thousand pounds. You'll need it pretty soon to pay for a plushy padded cell."

She sat motionless for a long while after he'd gone. She had no feelings at all; it was as though she'd been washed free of every emotion, been made clean, weightless. She knew she would sleep that night, but what she didn't know was whether the nightmares would come back again.

FOURTEEN

When the morning conference was over, Drummond beckoned Naylor into his office. Behind him was a sleepless night, lodged fast in his head a picture of his wife's pitiful face, blind-eyed and stupefied with non-belief, and in his ears the would-be consoling note in Tom Hardcliffe's voice as he'd handed him a copy of Juliet's bald, uncompromising statement.

"Frank, you're only one of a million parents who don't know their own kids because the kids don't want to be known. At least Juliet committed no offence with which the police can charge her, though she'll be called as a witness. It could have been worse, a whole lot worse. Try to believe that."

"You mean she might have been an accomplice to murder?"

"No, I mean that Ramsgate might have asked her to dispose of the silver for him."

Drummond's wrath and grief exploded out of his mouth: "My God, I couldn't feel much worse if she'd died."

He caught Tom's look of repugnance, knew it was earned, but didn't withdraw his words. "It'll half kill Meryl."

"I doubt it. Women are amazingly resilient. What's more, they automatically adjust to a situation they can't alter. Once Meryl's over the initial shock she may find it easier to come to terms with what's happened than you do."

His facial muscles clenched so tight his face looked carved out of some solid substance, he gave Naylor a cold, censorious glare. "You didn't contribute much, did you? You must have had some reaction from Ellis when you questioned him last night."

Naylor ignored the sneer, was careful not to show a flicker of sympathy, even understanding. "He could genuinely have forgotten Francis Clavering or Francis Clavering could have confused him with another guest, and even supposing he didn't make the side trip to Duchberry—and we haven't turned up anyone who saw him in the neighbourhood, much less spoke to him—the timing would have been tight. The folks at the pub in Outhwell confirm that he drove off from there between 5:15 and 5:30."

"Who's to say he arrived back at the hotel when he said he did, two A.M.? It could have been three, four. Later. He had his own key. There's no night porter."

"Agreed. But where's the motive?"

"The age-old one, money."

"I don't mean for the murder. I mean for making sure, given a bit of luck, we wouldn't be able to contact him for the best part of a week."

"Obvious. It would have given him ample time to dispose of a weapon and blood-stained clothing over several hundred square miles of country. We might as well look for a needle in a haystack. And the interval would serve to steady his nerves, always supposing he's got any. You know as well as I do, how a trail can cool in a week. And the older an alibi is, the harder it is to break."

Naylor, who had not been invited to sit down, commented: "All the same, sir, there's no hard proof." For instance, they had uncovered no positive sighting of the Cortina that Martin Ellis had used for his trip to the hotel in Leicestershire anywhere in the town or its environs on the Saturday night in question. His fingerprints had been found on the inside surface of the wardrobe he'd last used eight years ago, but nowhere else in the house. The only set of muddy footprints on the dining-room carpet fitted a pair of sneakers that Tony Ramsgate admitted wearing on the night Mervyn Ellis was murdered.

"Then get it, fast." Drummond, normally a man who would not demean his autocracy by losing his temper, hammered his fist on the desk. "It's there if you look for it. Go to that hotel, grill the staff till they squeal and then some more. I want every fact you can prise out of them on Martin Ellis. Does he usually spend his holidays alone hopping from one place to another. Check his bank account. Get a list of his unpaid bills, his outstanding commitments. And today, Stan."

In plain words, at any cost produce a strong suspect to stave off ultimate catastrophe: Juliet's boy friend being charged with murder.

"Will do. One other thing, sir, Tony Ramsgate's put in a request to see me. Apparently there's something he wants to add to his statement. He's due about now."

Drummond pressed a finger on the corner of his mouth to stop a vein twitching. "What's he want to add?"

"I won't know until I've seen him."

"Contact me as soon as you've finished with him."

"Yes, sir."

"And give orders for Francis Clavering to be brought by car from Launceston. We'll give him a sight of Ellis, get a positive identification."

Tony, normally thin as a length of string, had lost several pounds of flesh in three days. His blue eyes were fever-bright and his hair a good deal less clean than usual. He sat ramrod-straight in the chair, his spine making no contact with the back and announced in a dead flat voice: "I'm ready to talk."

"Glad to hear it," Naylor snapped. "Talk away."

"To talk about a deal," Tony enunciated carefully.

Naylor's smile was heavily sardonic. "You should know me better than to use that word to me. You've been reading too many detective novels. No deals in this station, Tony. Nor in any others I've ever heard of."

"In that case, you'd better ring for the police car to take me back to gaol."

"You've not seen the inside of a gaol yet. But you will. So talk. You've nothing to lose in disclosing your terms. Well, have you? So let's be hearing them."

Tony brooded, staring down at his hands that offended him because the nails were grimy, trying to work out what, aside from Juliet—who was already lost to him—he had at stake. He couldn't think of a thing. When the silence had lasted a whole minute, he brought himself to say: "I've got a girl. Her father is your boss."

"I've got more than one boss."

"Her name is Juliet Drummond."

"What part did she play in your little escapade, apart, of course, I take it, from being the bird in the car."

"That's all. She doesn't come into anything else."

What little colour Tony's face contained, drained out of it. The boy, Naylor decided, looked sick, but that was no one's fault but his own.

Tony went on, fighting to keep his voice steady, to ignore the great solid lumps of tears in his throat: "That's why she's got to be protected, kept out of this filthy business. I refuse to see her, admit I know her. If I'm questioned about her in the witness box, I'll swear on the Bible I've never seen her before."

"Perjury," Naylor commented, "is a criminal offence."

"You think I care!" His face ravaged by lack of sleep, inability to eat the coarse food that was served up to him, seemed to take on a pale glow. "There's nothing any of you can do to me that will make me admit that I've ever seen or spoken to Juliet Drummond. That way, the fuzz won't be able to pin anything on her."

"Look, boy, martyrdom went out of fashion a good few centuries ago. Juliet Drummond's got a tongue in her head, hasn't she? There might be things she could say in your defence. Wouldn't she want to say them?"

"She's not to be given a chance. Anyway, it will be her word against mine."

"So what do you want me to do? What's this deal of yours?"

"Stop her coming to see me at the Remand Centre. Issue an order that she's not to be admitted. That lawyer has promised to do his best, but she'll ignore him. I know her. But a police order, she couldn't ignore that, could she? And I don't want her coming into court."

"And if I decided to issue such an order, what's your end of the deal?"

"Nothing until you've given me a promise."

"You're too late, son. Juliet Drummond has made a full statement to us through her father's solicitor. She's admitted being in your company in a stolen car on the night Mervyn Ellis was murdered and she's been picked out by a witness in an identity parade. Among other things, she has in her possession two tickets to Katmandu, one in her name, one in yours, and, what's more, she's been . . . well . . . explicit about the relationship that exists between you." He paused, to give Tony a breather from the shocks raining on him, before he went on: "Your Juliet is the only child of Superintendent Drummond and you can safely leave him to provide any protection she needs. He's exceptionally well placed to ensure she gets all she's entitled to."

"He'll crucify her," Tony moaned. "So will her mum."

"I doubt it. Her parents have had thirty-six hours to absorb the shock; any time now they'll begin to emerge from it and start acting like normal parents of an only child. From all accounts Juliet Drummond is a girl with a will of her own, used to getting her own way; not the type to appreciate you making deals behind her back. So come on, let's be having it." When Tony, gritting his teeth to keep the tears behind his lids, didn't answer, he went on: "I'd be prepared to hazard a guess. You've remembered exactly where you found the silver."

The tears beat him, drowned him under successive waves of humiliation. It was a full minute, during which Naylor waited with stoical patience, before he regained his voice.

Charles Palfrey spent half a minute of concentrated study on Elaine Lowther. His verdict, that she was a responsible, conscientious young woman but, that as a spinster at thirty or thereabouts, there was possibly a streak of frustrated motherhood in her. Anyway, the total of what she'd been at some pains to relate to him added up to precious little.

"But you haven't actually been in contact with Tony Ramsgate for some time. How long exactly?"

"Four and a half years." The suggestion of belittlement in his tone stung her. "He can't have turned vicious and brutal in that short while. His whole nature isn't likely to have changed so violently, surely?"

Charles Palfrey had known natures to change in far less time, but he refrained from saying so. He looked over his notes, gave her his best professional smile marred only by a tinge of impatience. "I'm grateful to you for making a deposition on my client's behalf. It may well prove of value. You are aware, I imagine that so far he has only been charged with the theft of a car, plus certain articles of silver which he sold knowing they had been stolen?"

"Yes, but it's not impossible that he might be charged with a much more serious offence?"

His smile this time was superior. "We mustn't be pessimistic at this stage."

Since he obviously expected her to rise, she did so. At the door she paused, asked: "Is he allowed visitors? Would it be possible for me to see him?"

"It would be possible except that he has stated categorically that he doesn't wish to see any, not even his mother. That's his privilege, you know, and we must respect it."

"Even so, I'd like him to know that I *asked* if I could see him. Would you tell him, and mention where I met him, at the Youth Club four and a half years ago? He may not recall my name, but I think there's a chance he might remember me. Would you do this next time you see him?"

He promised, but so casually that she doubted whether he would keep his word.

Her route back to the office took her by the police station. She walked past it and then, her mind resolving itself, turned about and retraced her steps.

The young sergeant at the desk who'd taken part in the house-to-house enquiries along Hartfield Road, recognised her. "It's Miss Lowther, isn't it? What can I do for you, miss?"

"Would you ask Sergeant Naylor if I could see him?"

"I'm afraid he's not here today, miss. He may be back tomorrow though it's not certain. Is there any way that I can help?"

Her hand in her coat pocket, her fingers clenched round the ball-point pen, she experienced a sense of let-down that was like falling from a state of grace into impenetrable darkness. With no warning belief fought non-belief until it seemed she was riven into two persons.

The young sergeant leaned across the desk. "Are you all right, miss? Like me to get you a drink of water?"

She shook her head. The blackness was passing. It had been silly to get into such a state because Inspector Naylor wasn't available. She could talk to another officer, but now all desire to do so had left her. She said quietly: "Thank you. I'm all right now. I'll look in and see if Inspector Naylor is here tomorrow."

By the time she reached the office, the curious, inexplicable spasm, though not the memory of it, had passed. On her desk were a pile of typed messages. The top one read:

1:45 *p.m.*
Miss Pilkington's nephew telephoned. Miss Pilkington wishes him to see over Quarry Vale House

before she finally decides whether she will buy the property. He is driving her over tomorrow afternoon (Wednesday) and asks if you would meet them there at 5 o'clock with the keys to the house.

Robert's most direct route home, after interviewing a sixty-two-year-old grandmother who had been a secret painter all her married life and had astounded her family by winning an international prize, took him down Hartfield Road. He slowed the car at the curb, the urge to spend time—even fruitless time—while it remained to spend so strong as to be irresistible. In a little over three weeks the odds were he'd never see Elaine again.

Her car was standing in the open garage, but when he rang the bell, it went unanswered. Loath to accept the sharp cut of disappointment, he walked round the house, stood on the rear terrace gazing down the stretch of lawn to a high trellis of roses. She was standing on tiptoe striving to reach a wildly spiralling branch. In the warm, golden evening light he was content to have her in sight, to stay motionless and look his fill.

A sharp cry of annoyance or pain cut through the air. He strode forward, found her sucking the palm of her hand.

"Here, let me look."

"It's only a thorn." She gave him her hand, her smile for once freely welcoming, happily startled. "What did you do, fall out of a moon rocket."

He competently extracted the thorn. "Now all you have to do is to put it under a running tap. No, I stopped by as I had to pass your door to ask if you'd like me to pick you up for Rosie's party tomorrow night."

"I might be late. I'm meeting a client at Quarry Vale House at five. It's a hideous tumble-down maze. If I get out by 6:30 I'll be lucky. I doubt if I'll be ready to leave here before eight."

"Then we'll both be late. With the number of guests Rosie has invited, no one will miss us."

"It's a final fling. Her parents arrive home from Canada next week. Mrs Chard is a tidy soul."

"I know, I've met her. Plumps up the cushions almost before you're on your feet."

She laughed. Her hair was tousled, and there was a smear of blood on her chin that he found endearing. He glanced from her to the rampaging branches. "What you need on that job is a man with a saw!"

"They're out of hand, have been for years. I nearly had them dug up last autumn." She gave them a wry look. "Frau Druschka. Mother's favourites. To Dad they were sacred."

"But he's been dead . . . how long?"

"Five years." Her smile was self-mocking. "So why haven't I had them dug up! Because I could never bring myself to the point of decision whether to stay here or move. Sheer lazy-mindedness."

"If you didn't stay, where would you go?"

"Anywhere, I suppose. There's no rule of life that compels me to work for Robson & Bates until I'm old enough to draw a pension. I could find another job, even have none at all for a while."

His grave, yet frighteningly hopeful expression, forced her into instant retreat. "More likely I shall sell this house, and buy another in Coldbridge, or a modern flat, one of my own choice, not just a relic of the past."

"A splendid idea. Don't go back on it. Elaine, I mean that. But why not leave Coldbridge?"

She hedged, her eyes turning evasive. "I don't think I could. Not yet."

"Why not?" he pressed, wanting to know, feeling that there might lie the button that would unlock the mystery of Elaine.

"I can't explain. I'm terribly bad at explaining myself." Her throat moved, and she said in a tumble of harsh words:

"I was born here, thirty years ago. Sometimes I get scared I'll die here."

"Elaine, love. For God's sake!"

His distress had the effect of sending her behind her wall of glass, terrified she'd made a shameful exhibition of herself. She laughed on a curious high, strained note. "Sorry. I didn't mean it. It was a line from a play I once saw years ago." Abruptly, she changed the subject. "If you'll make them we'll have a jug of ice-cold dry martinis. Will you, while I clean myself up?"

Experience had taught him there was no quick reprieve against the withdrawal from which, for a little while, no coaxing could win her back. "It'd be a pleasure," he said drily.

With dress and shoes changed, hair smooth, she took the glass from him, said: "I saw Mr Palfrey this morning. I don't think I made much of an impression on him. Oh, he was polite enough, made a note of what I said, but I left with the impression he thought I was wasting his time discussing what wasn't my business."

"He's a smug, pompous little man, but what you said can't have done Ramsgate any harm."

She gave him a shrewd look. "But even you think the time-gap is too wide for anything I say to be any help to Tony, don't you?"

"A character reference is of more value if it's current, not over four years out of date."

The stubborn look came back to her face. "But he didn't commit murder."

"Because you claim at the age of fifteen he was nauseated by the sight of blood!"

"He didn't do it."

His professional curiosity leaped high. For the space of half a minute she ceased to be a woman who at some moments he loved, at all moments cared for, and was transformed into the magic touchstone for an exclusive story.

"There's got to be some reason why you're so positive Ramsgate is innocent. It's my belief you're hiding some piece of evidence that you haven't revealed to the police. Aren't I right?"

She looked at him with alarm, then shook her head, twice. "You're wrong."

"I don't think I am," he said firmly. "I think you're what, in legal talk, is an accessory after the fact—the fact of murder."

"You're making up a story in your head to fit the headlines you want to use."

She was obstinate, he thought, obstinate and secretive, half of her wrapped tight out of sight; at the same time he wondered drearily how long it would take him to wipe her from memory.

"About Ramsgate," he said, giving up interrogating her, because bitter experience had proved it futile, "I went to see his mother this morning. She maintains it's a simple case of mistaken identity, and isn't even prepared to concede he stole the car or the silver, though he admits to both offences. She's a fiercely respectable little woman, with a flat shined up fit to receive the Queen. It seems her husband deserted her when Tony was a baby and it's my guess she's slaved for him ever since, made him her *raison d'être* for living. The point I'm trying to make is that's a pretty lousy burden to hang round any boy's neck. Maybe he just couldn't take the load any longer." He paused. "The vast majority of murders aren't premeditated. They're the end product of mental explosions. The supreme act of desperation to release years of frustration."

"You're trying to convince me that Tony went berserk and battered an old man to death to escape from the clutches of an overpossessive mother! You haven't succeeded and you never will."

"Fair enough, you won't confide in me because you believe, mistakenly as it happens, that any fact—even suspicion—you passed to me, would be banner-headlined in the *Argus*." He leaned far enough forward to grasp her free hand. He hung onto it. "All right, go to the police. Naylor or Drummond, Naylor for preference. Even if it's only the vaguest suspicion. Elaine!" He squeezed the hand so hard, that she drew in her breath. "Sorry, but I'm deadly serious. Give me your promise, love."

She shook her head. "What a bore and a bother I am. Not worth all the trouble. You should go out of the front door and forget I exist."

"I can't. I don't want to. That promise. Come on. Naylor. You've only got to lift the phone."

"Tomorrow. He's away or off-duty until then."

"Why not Drummond, or there's Skilley?"

"I'll wait for Inspector Naylor."

Standing outside the gate he'd closed behind him, he waited until she'd switched off all the lights except the one in her bedroom. He walked up the road, and then down again four times, and at the end of half an hour the house was in darkness. Then, taking off his shoes, so that his feet made no sound on the path, he tested the lock on the front door, checked that the back door was secured, and that the latches on the downstairs windows were fastened.

Unless an intruder risked the noise of shattering glass in a quiet built-up area, or resorted to a ladder to reach her open bedroom window, she was safe for the night. But safe from whom? Who the hell did he think was going to molest her? By the time he'd downed a treble Scotch in the misnamed easy chair in his bedroom, he'd rationalised the security check as an outside anxiety complex over a girl who was secretive to the point of neuroticism. But, if she'd kept whatever information on Ellis's murder she was withholding from him, would she have confided in anyone else? He decided, no. Even so, he slept fitfully. At nine o'clock he rang Police Headquarters, asked when Naylor was expected back in Coldbridge, and was told some time in the late afternoon.

He left an urgent message asking Naylor to contact him as soon as he reached his office. That way, he could send him to Elaine, instead of waiting for Elaine to report to Naylor, give her a chance to change her mind. Or have it changed for her.

FIFTEEN

There was release from the miseries of a trip-wire existence in taking a piece of the future and shaping it to his own pattern. The sheer exhilaration of having control over events speeded Martin's wits as he mapped out a time-table, checked and rechecked it in his head. It was a soothing process that dissolved the last fumes of rage and left him in a state of calm that was near impregnable. The day and its outcome took on a semblance of predestination, a goal towards which he had been advancing since his teens. A just, right finishing.

He left the house at 5 A.M., returned two and a half hours later and, satisfied with the outcome of his explorations, cooked himself a substantial breakfast. During the morning he changed his clothes, packed his bag and stowed it in the car boot.

Around noon he telephoned Police Headquarters and asked for Inspector Naylor. Sergeant Tanner informed him Naylor wasn't available, and enquired if he could take a message. Martin said he was vacating the house late that afternoon after handing over the keys to Mr Cheetham of Robson & Bates. Sergeant Tanner asked for his London address and telephone number in order that Inspector Naylor could contact him. Martin replied that they were already on record; Tanner had merely to look them up. Tanner then asked for his estimated time of arrival in London. Martin considering this no business of Tanner's, replied vaguely some time before midnight.

Twice during the morning and once after lunch he rang Sheila's number. There was no reply. The last time he kept the receiver to his ear for a full five minutes, painting a series of pictures in his mind: the car driving up to the empty house, Sheila slotting her key into the lock, and running so fast down the hall that her voice when she answered was breathless. None materialised. The deadening sense of let-down returned, the worms of suspicion that mocked his love threatened to undermine him, but he thrust them fiercely away. The day itself, with its climax that would spell a release from a life-sentence, served as a dynamo to boost him back into euphoric calm.

When Kenneth Cheetham collected the keys he did not ask him inside the house, but handed them over the door-step. When Cheetham showed a disposition to linger and boast of the buyers he had lined up, Martin briskly excused himself on the score of last-minute clearing up to do before he left for London. He was, he said, aiming to be on his way by five.

He closed the door behind him at 3:45. Instead of driving down Hartfield Road he turned right, along a route that would take him past the minimum of neighbours who might chance to mark his departure, and led him into the stream of traffic leaving the town.

A mile and a half from Quarry Vale House he stopped, unlatched a gate which opened into a firebreak cut through a Forestry Commission plantation of conifers. When he was invisible from the road, he found a space where, with some manoeuvring, he could turn the car. A marginal risk existed that the Rover might be marked and remembered, but in the dense afforestation of well-established but not yet mature trees, the chance of a Forestry workman or inspector passing that way within the next couple of hours was minimal. And even if one did, as he was parked in a right-of-way, there'd be no reason for anyone to record the number of the car.

When he'd walked back to the road, the temptation to

make one more examination of the steep unguarded bank below the bridge over the river was near irresistible, but his schedule was too tightly drawn to permit of that little indulgence. Also one of the underpins of his plan was to escape notice by chance passers-by.

Two interlocking lanes led him to the sheep moor which ran down from the blind man's cottage that was within five minutes' walk of Quarry Vale House. He had covered half the distance when the cottage door was flung open and the dog came bounding towards him, barking ferociously.

Through a thin gathering mist Martin observed that the blind man was short, squat, with wisps of light-coloured hair plastered to his forehead. He cupped his hands in the shape of a trumpet, shouted, but the distance between them swallowed all but the last word ". . . there?"

As the blind man started down the path, the dog raced towards Martin. He bent, picked up a stone and hurled it. The dog, hit on the foreleg, yelped, paused momentarily and then launched itself forward, fangs bared. A long, low whistle stopped it dead in its tracks.

The blind man was only a dozen yards away. He too had stopped, was shouting: "Scout! Scout!" and then: "Who's there? What do you want?"

If he ran, the dog would run after him, outrun him, have the seat out of his pants, maybe leap for his throat. The delay he hadn't reckoned with that, if protracted, would wreck his timetable, panicked him. For a few seconds his mind darkened with the ultimate in catastrophes: Elaine winning —his personal nemesis left free to torment and threaten him forevermore. He had to steady himself with a reminder that the man was blind. Totally blind, according to Sheila. He gazed at the thick-set, strong body, the creased, weather-beaten face, the wide-open bright blue eyes. It needed an effort of will, the fact that the eyes were not quite focused on him, but to his left, to convince him that the man had but four senses—and only one that mattered a damn: ears. All that was required of him was an easy trick—one he'd been adept at since his schooldays, and had found useful in amateur dramatics in South Africa, mimicry. He adopted the whining tone of a working-class town youth. "Call him off, please, mister. I ain't done nothing. I was only taking a short-cut to the Sheffield bus, and he goes for me. I'm not doing any harm, only keeping to the path. If you don't call him off I'm likely to miss my bus."

The blind man shouted back in an angry, obstinate voice: "This is private land; you've no business to be on it. Scout was doing his duty chasing off trespassers. I heard you throw a stone. Serve you right if he'd got you." He called the dog to heel, fondled its head, ran his hand carefully over its quarters. "I've a good mind to call the police."

Martin silently scoffed. With no telephone that was an empty threat. All he had to do was wheedle: "Mister, if I'm on private property, I'm sorry, but I didn't see a sign. If you hold the dog off, I'll be away as fast as my feet can take me."

"Then get along, and keep moving." He bent, gripped the dog's collar. "And don't let me catch you round these parts again, or I'll have Scout pen you up until the police get here."

"I'm on my way, mister."

He ran as soft-footed as he could to the bottom of the moor, though the wall there was higher, more difficult to scale than farther up. But the hearing of the blind is said to be more acute than the normal man's to compensate for loss of sight and, for all he knew, the blind shepherd had ears like a bat.

His cover, picked out soon after dawn, was ready and waiting: a niche in the rampant growth of rhododendrons that overflowed on to both sides of the drive. For a moment, squatting on his haunches on the damp leafmould, he had to reassure himself that the great thumping beats of his heart were no more than the physical effect of the long sprint across the hummocky sheep pasture, the scrambling leap over the wall. Thanks to the quickness of his reaction, the plan—which he saw in his mind as an intricate, inter-laced map—was not disrupted. In fact, he was five minutes early.

His confidence rock-hard, he took the gun from the pocket of his trenchcoat. He had, in South Africa, where private arms are common, handled both rifles and revolvers, though he had never possessed a gun of his own until a fortnight ago when the tool to kill had been literally put into his hands by his milk-sop father.

There was another source of irony which served to while away the last five minutes. When a beneficiary to a will was dead and without kin, as Elaine was—both her mother and her father being only children—as residual legatee the thousand pounds she'd never intended to give him would naturally revert to him. As he nipped off care-fully selected leaves to make himself a wider peephole in the jungle growth of rhododendrons, he was inwardly con-vulsed with triumphant glee.

He'd no need to see down the drive, which was a curve anyway, only obliquely to his left, where his target was a flight of corroded stone steps leading to a door that had once been white but which was now grey-green with mould.

At two minutes to five he heard her car turn through the gate, and the last but one uncertainty was erased: that Elaine might have telephoned Miss Pilkington. The drive was potholed, narrowed by untrimmed shrubs and seedling trees. Even Elaine's Mini had to proceed cautiously. Wait-ing, his mind luxuriated in penetrating five minutes into the future. He saw her in an obscene sprawl at the base of the steps, dead, or if not dead, at the mercy of his *coup de grâce*. He had condemned her to death, not because of the puerile nonsense of the ball-point pen. Even if she took it to the police, the evidence was too flimsy to provide a spring-board for suspicion. No, the error that had cost her her life was her assumption that she still held the power to menace and coerce him into the subservience of the past. It was really a very simple equation: as long as she lived, he'd never be free of fear. Weird, he was prepared to admit, but then Elaine was weird, always had been, with a mind that was either unsound or sick.

The blue Mini emerged from the curve and until he could verify with his own eyes that she was alone, the last shadow of doubt hung between him and the certainty of release. She was.

Ten yards, say a minute and a half to drive to the steps, get out of the car, find the key in her handbag, slot it into the lock, and be posed with her back to him. That the last few seconds of her life were running out of him put a sweetness on his tongue, a bottomless joy in his heart. It marked the end of the death feud that stretched back into their childhood.

He watched with a silent scream of agonising disbelief as the car, instead of stopping at the bottom of the crumbling steps, merely slowed down to take the angle of the house, and disappeared from sight.

With an old-fashioned, unwieldy key Elaine unlocked the back door—the lock on the front door being faulty, it was kept bolted on the inside. To reach the hall she had to pass through an interlocking chain of sculleries and cavernous kitchens, the smell of mould, dry rot and the disintegrating bodies of insects and small rodents heavy in her nostrils. Although, thanks to Miss Pilkington, she knew her way about the house blindfold, cobwebs that were newly spun since her last visit glutinously coated her hair and skin.

Reaching the hall from which the staircase rose to a galleried first floor, she forced back the stubborn bolt and left the front door ajar for Miss Pilkington and nephew. The four main reception rooms had fine hand-carved mahogany doors that, except for the verdigris on the filigree brass fitments, had withstood the onslaught of damp and decay. She noticed that a mist was beginning to rise from the moors spreading tentacles of vapour towards the house, setting objects at a distance, and to bring more light into the hall where the windows were opaque with grime, she parted all the doors and flung them open.

Then she checked her watch. Miss Pilkington, obsessively punctual, was actually five minutes late! It would appear that Peregrine didn't calculate time in split seconds. There being nowhere to sit downstairs, she climbed to the main bedroom, which had a box-seat fitted below the window. She cleaned a pane with tissue to give her a view of the drive and settled down to wait.

She was staring abstractedly at a cracked moulded cornice in which two cherubs gambolled with floating scarves when her ear, alert for the sound of Miss Pilkington's car, heard the creak of a floorboard, followed by the pad of a cautious footstep somewhere below on the ground floor.

The risk of vagrants or squatters breaking into the house had always existed; so much so that at one time Kenneth had considered boarding up the ground-floor windows, then decided against it as, with the electricity cut off, prospective clients would have had to inspect the reception rooms by torchlight.

She bent her head forward, listened with concentration and decided that the stealthy footfalls with pauses in between emanated from the hall. Her first reaction was one of exasperation that she'd probably be embroiled in an ugly scene with an intruder when Miss Pilkington arrived; also that somewhere in the house was a smashed window for Miss Pilkington to gloat over.

To learn the size and sex of the intruder she kicked off her shoes and crept to the door. She had left it half-open and there was a vein of light down the jamb; narrow, admittedly, but by pressing her eye to it she could get a sight of him—or it could be a woman, even a child—before "it" began to climb the stairs.

At first she saw only the hand clasping a gun appear round the dining-room door, followed by half of Martin,

167

not quite prepared to abandon his cover. For an instant the shock of his appearance was such that she was momentarily stupefied. The blankness of mind passed, leaving her wrapped in a calm so absolute that it placed her temporarily beyond the reach of fear, while she savoured a strange, clinical satisfaction. She had yearned for proof, and there, down a single flight of stairs, it was presented to her. Martin was prepared to hunt her down, a gun in his hand, rather than risk her handing over to the police a piece of evidence that would not stand up in any court in the land. The real evidence, of the mind and the senses, had no substance.

In a dreamlike fashion, like creating a fantasy, she speculated on the method by which he proposed to dispose of her body when he'd killed her. Bury her in the soft leaf-mould in one of the shrubberies that shrouded the house? Drop her down the well? Drag her corpse up to the moors and inter it under an outcrop of stones? Her immediate emotional reaction was not terror, rather a sense of meeting head-on a stupendous challenge in which the initial advantage lay with her in that she could see him, while he had to seek her out in an unfamiliar house with twenty rooms.

She waited until he emerged from the dining room and then did a quick survey of the space behind her. Even if she'd been prepared to commit herself to a trap, there was no cupboard, not even a projection to give her cover: simply four bare walls with two doors, neither of which possessed a key. As she heard his footfall cautiously mount the first stair, her eye fastened on the second door. It led into a dressing room almost as large as the bedroom, its outer door opening on to the landing, but at a point where it was not visible until anyone climbing the stairs reached the gallery.

She slid through it, across the landing, and up the steep servants' staircase that led to the attics, remembering too late her shoes that provided evidence of her presence on the first floor and, since she hadn't descended the staircase, a signpost to the direction she'd taken.

Halfway up the boarded-in staircase she thought she

heard the sound of a car in the drive. Miss Pilkington! A second later an appalling certainty ripped through her head. The phone message had been a hoax! Simple as pie for someone like Martin with a small talent for mimicry. She leant against the boarding, her confidence momentarily sapped by the ease with which he'd tricked and manipulated her. It was the soft squeak of a stair that whipped up her resolution. Thanks to Miss Pilkington's indefatigable viewings of the property she remembered which of the five attics would provide her with an escape route. Beyond the sash window was a rudimentary fire escape, so rust-eroded that the lower half had come adrift and lay in a mangled heap of old iron in the stable yard. But the upper section functioned: Miss Pilkington had proved it by gripping its rail and tugging hard before she trusted her substantial weight to it for the purpose of inspecting the roof which was single-span, slate, like a grey tent, the whole encircled by a toy-sized plaster balustrade, lengths of which had broken away, guarding a narrow catwalk.

Miss Pilkington's well-muscled legs had climbed up the fire escape with the confidence of one who had been a mountaineer in her youth, proclaiming into the wind that you could only judge the soundness of the roof from the outside. Elaine had proposed to remain in the attic, but Miss Pilkington would have none of it. "No head for heights, is it! Only one cure for that, my girl, get up top. Come along. I'll need you to keep count of the loose slates."

So Elaine, her hair blowing in her eyes, had scrambled on to the catwalk just as Miss Pilkington had pried the first slate loose and sent it spinning to earth.

On that day the window had responded to one upward thrust. Now it stuck and Elaine needed all her muscle power to raise it. She was still balancing herself with one hand on the sill, as she steadied her shoeless feet on a rung of the fire escape, when the sash snapped, and the slamming frame struck her little finger.

The pain made her movements laboured and clumsy.

When at last she reached the catwalk, clinging to a length of balustrade for support, vertigo attacked her, and memory blanked out: she couldn't remember in which direction Miss Pilkington had turned, left or right. She was lost and made utterly helpless by a mental fog. It was the damp clamminess of her skin that revived her. Not a mental fog, but mist drifting in from the moors, in light swathes, like opaque scarves that were parted and pulled together again by the wind. One moment she could see a chimney stack; the next it was blotted out.

Her objective was a ladder hanging on the wall at one side of the house reaching from the guttering to the ground. Criminal negligence, Miss Pilkington had dubbed it, an open invitation to burglars. If he had been in her employ the minion who had left it suspended there would have been summarily dismissed. Its purpose, naturally, was to afford instant access to the roof in heavy snow, but the snow cleared, it should have been removed, placed under lock and key.

Elaine was jerked into motion by the bang of the attic window as it slammed shut a second time. The shoes had given her away. Now she was positive that the ladder hung on the west wall, so she must turn right. The catwalk, silted with the sodden skeletons of a dozen winters' leaves, was skiddy under her nylon-clad feet. No sooner had she scrambled ten yards than she became equally positive she'd chosen the wrong direction, which meant she would either have to circle the whole roof, or retrace her steps. As she stood without moving, willing her brain to take the decision, somewhere behind in the eerie stillness, she heard a metallic click. In slow motion she twisted her head, prepared to gaze into an opaqueness that drowned outlines, swallowed whole objects, and instead found herself looking down a channel of light that the wind must have cleared. At the end of it Martin was in the act of raising a revolver.

She stood wordless, paralysed as in a nightmare, not from fear, but the palpitating hatred that was a living, breathing element in the space between them. Hatred that her obsessive, abject love had bred in its recipient. For a moment she was plunged into darkness, then out of that darkness spiralled a certainty so absolute that she shouted it aloud: "You killed your father. You beat him to death."

He jeered back: "The old fool had lived too long. It was time he was dead. The same goes for you."

Her eye measured his hand rise another inch, and with a wholly reflex action she threw herself round a sharp angle of the roof. There was a flash, a screaming sound like none she had ever heard before as a slate shattered into dust before her eyes. Clawing frantically at a stumpy length of balustrade that crumbled as she hung on to it, she regained her feet, but all she could manage was a shuffling run that was a futile waste of effort when measured against the running steps pursuing her. She thought, I could crawl quicker, and fell to her hands and knees, grovelling among the silt and filth of the catwalk.

A yelp, more animal-like than human, froze her where she crouched. And, while she crouched, there was a softer, almost imperceptible sound of air being displaced. When she could bring herself to look behind her, there was nothing but space and thin wisps of mist that interlaced and then parted company.

Slowly, painfully the ladder hanging from the wall surfaced in her head, an objective she must reach, and to find it she must somehow regain her feet. When she did so, she swayed. After a small eternity of mindless exploring, she sighted it suspended a good two foot below the parapet. To lever her muscleless legs backwards over the low wall seemed an impossible feat to accomplish, but slowly the lead-heavy limbs obeyed her will, and her feet curled round the rungs of the ladder that cut into her bare feet. Rung after rung, they were uncountable, a purgatory that would never end. She still had another ten to find when two arms grasped her waist.

A voice furious, indignant, and frightened out of its wits

screeched: "What the hell's going on? You doing some sort of dance of death round the roof with a maniac! For God's sake, what would have happened to you if I hadn't been a demon bowler? That's all I could do, pick up the nearest rock and aim for his head."

She leaned against him, slowly found sufficient strength to turn her head and look into Graham Cheetham's chalk-white face. He added, his mouth shaking: "Lucky for you, I didn't miss. Me, too, maybe. He might have taken a pot-shot at me."

She asked in a small but perfectly steady voice: "Where is he?"

Events had moved too fast and too horrifically for Graham. He was way out of his depth, robbed of coherent thought. He pointed in the direction of the well. "Don't go near him. I don't know whether he's dead or alive, nor where the gun is. Keep clear."

When she did not heed him, he pulled on her arm. But at that moment in time she was stronger than he was.

Elaine crouched on the hard cobbles, found the flicker of a pulse, looked up at Graham who was distractedly hovering over her, babbling something about Miss Pilkington having telephoned and asked Elaine to meet her at the house on Friday, and stoutly denying that her nephew had telephoned to make an appointment for Wednesday. And Kenneth sending him haring off so that Elaine shouldn't hang about waiting to keep a date that had never been made.

She cut across his gabble of words. "There's not likely to be a telephone nearer than the stone house just before you reach the crossroads. Hurry. Telephone for an ambulance. Tell them it's urgent."

"And leave you here with a gun-happy maniac hell-bent on bloody murder! Not likely. You're coming with me."

She said so fiercely that he flinched: "Graham, get going. I'm staying here. Move."

He blinked, employed another delaying tactic. "I'm not

172

leaving you here alone with him until I've found the gun. For all we know he may be shamming, putting on a big act, waiting to have another go at murdering you. What the hell is it all about anyway?"

She shouted: "He's got a broken leg, in all probability a fractured skull."

"He damn well deserves both. *When* I find the gun, I'll phone for an ambulance, but I shall take it with me."

She found it for him, half hidden beneath the rotting cover of the well that Miss Pilkington had tipped onto the ground with the ferrule of her stick. Only then would he be coerced into the car, the gun beside him on the seat. Driving off he gave her a look that suggested he doubted whether he'd ever see her alive again.

When she could no longer hear the car, she knelt with her bruised knees on the iron hard cobblestones. He scarcely breathed, his pulse was now barely perceptible, and blood seeped round one ear, followed the line of his jaw and dripped into his collar.

As she watched, his eyes, their strange colour muted and clouded, shadows of themselves, opened. He saw her face, but it revolved in triplicate, three separate images that coalesced into one, and then separated again.

He had no consciousness of physical pain, only a searing agony of heart and mind that Elaine was alive when she should have been a corpse at the bottom of the well, her Mini with its doors open submerged under the bridge over the river that was thirty feet deep at that point. Alive! His lips parted and two words broke softly but distinctly from his throat: "She devil . . ."

She watched the lids stiffen round the staring eyes. She closed them, rose with labour to her feet and leant for support against the wellhead. The death duel was resolved. In a way, she thought, I killed him.

SIXTEEN

In the interview room where they sat on opposite sides of a small plastic table, a warder on guard at the door, Juliet lowered her voice to a passionate hiss. "All right, so you'll go to prison for a few months. That's what Charles Palfrey says, a year at the most, with time off for good behaviour. What's a few months out of a whole lifetime? It's a nothing. A nothing."

To him the most astounding, most frightening aspect of the visit, was that she had not changed. The past week had left no visible mark on her. She was the same girl who had sat with him in the borrowed car that Saturday night. He shifted his gaze from the pale amber hair, the wide, speedwell blue eyes. "You call stealing from a dead man a nothing?"

"You stole for me, for both of us. He was dead. A corpse couldn't miss what you stole. You did it for us, Tony. For two people made one for the rest of their lives."

His heart no longer stirred to the oft-repeated words; it was as though they were a refrain he'd learnt in childhood and half forgotten. He relived the scene he had spied through the open French window that was embossed on his memory for all time: the foul, blood-splattered bed, the hideous stiffening corpse, the table lamp that, still alight, had tumbled onto the floor, flooding half the room with brightness, and illuminating the glittering silver that lay within his hand's grasp. He smelt the blood in his nostrils, and although his lips did not move, his stomach retched.

To break the silence that was a pain, he asked too loudly: "How's it with your parents?"

She shrugged impatience. "I wouldn't know. It doesn't matter. I'm leaving home." She leaned towards him, smiling tentatively. "You remember Jane? Jane Murphy."

He shook his head.

"Yes, you do," she countered. "I pointed her out to you in a coffee bar, back in the summer. She's got a job teaching in Manchester and her own flat. What's more, she's willing to share with me, and I'll get a job too." She sounded as uplifted as though she were about to embark on a great adventure. "And I've sent the tickets back to the travel agent and had them credited. We can claim new ones any time we want. I shall write and order them weeks before you're released so that we won't waste a moment taking off."

He wondered if all women, under the skin, were built to an identical mould, refusing to acknowledge a truth if it did not suit them. Juliet and his mother united in uncrackable faith or immutable obstinacy! His mother's idiot refrain that he was taking the blame for someone else. That it was not he who'd entered the room on an impulse of greed, grabbed the silver and run. Juliet and her nothing! For one awesome, horrifying moment he saw a likeness to his mother on Juliet's face.

She leaned across the table, picked up his hand, held it between her two tiny ones. "Tony, love, my love, it's the same today as that evening I met you coming out of the movies and because you weren't looking where you were going, my umbrella nearly poked your eye out! Don't you remember, that's when it happened, like beautiful music or a song written specially for us." She lifted the flaccid hand, kissed it, and whispered: "Remember the barn?"

He remembered the barn, but it bore no relation to the present he was living, or his future that was to be a prison. Katmandu and the Great Barrier Reef had become as faint and fading as a long-ago dream. He'd not only ceased to believe in a bus ride to the foothills of the Himalayas but he had ceased to believe in love. And that love, so splendid, so transfiguring, had died in him made him want to weep, but his eyes stayed dry.

She released his hand, put up a fingertip to trace his mouth. He was touched by a whisper of the old, melting tenderness, but in a second it had gone. She coaxed: "Don't go so far away from me. I keep you near me all the time. Even when I'm asleep, I know you're there, with me."

He moved his head, so that her finger was left in space, blurted out: "I don't want you to wait for me. I don't want you to be tied to an ex-convict."

She gave a high laugh that had a phony semblance of gaiety. "Big deal, when you don't have any say. I choose who I wait for."

Anger drove him to disregard the listening ear at the door, to shout: "And you've no need to leave your home and doting parents on my account."

"Oh, I'm not." She gave him a lofty smile. "I can't wait to leave home. Actually Daddy's relieved, though he'd never admit it. I've tarnished the image of his baby-daughter, so the sooner I'm out of sight the less painful it will be. And Mummy will adjust as long as I remember to telephone her once a week and convince her I'm neither starving nor smoking pot."

But would his mother readjust, he wondered despairingly, or would her cross and his weigh heavier with each passing year? He could leave her—in a way he was doing that now—but could he ever forget her? Even be given the chance. Every visiting day she'd be there, a martyr vehemently proclaiming his innocence, digging in her tartan hold-all bag for the walnut creams he'd liked as a child but detested now.

He noted the warder by the door glancing at his watch. He checked his own. Only one minute of the allotted half hour remained.

He gave her a lingering glance in which compassion, poignant nostalgia and fear mingled, said with all the depth of fervour of which he was capable: "Forget me. That's all I ask, forget we ever met."

For a second her nostrils quivered, and a look of animal fright darted through her eyes, but in another it was gone. "I couldn't if I tried, so I don't intend to waste time trying. I shall be in court on Monday. I'll come and see you every visiting day, and when you're released from whatever prison they send you to, I'll be waiting for you at the gate, the bus tickets to Katmandu in my pocket."

The warder made a discreet signal. She stood up, hesitated, the stricken look back, pinching her face. Then she banished it with a superbly confident smile. "I shan't forget you, nor give you the chance of forgetting me." She looked as though she was going to bend and kiss him, then she changed her mind, walked away from him and through the door the warder held open for her without a backward glance. That was what had first attracted him to her, her walk, light, upright, perfectly balanced, like that of a royal princess.

For a moment he almost believed her words; in another moment belief was dead.

When Robert telephoned to ask Elaine if they could meet on Saturday evening and, if so, what she would like to do, she chose a Sibelius concert being given by a visiting symphony orchestra. That he had not known she enjoyed classical music added extra weight to his hopelessness. Whole areas of each of them were unknown to the other. For instance, she didn't know he was a Boswell fan, that he'd been a champion boy swimmer, and that his favourite relaxation was to do absolutely nothing but stare at the sky. For reference his mind dragged itself back eight years—to when he and Lucille had been falling in love—but, for God's sake, that had ended in total disaster.

As the concert began at seven, he booked a table for a late supper at The Three Kings. Driving down Hartfield Road he wished he knew—could even begin to hazard a guess—of the effect on Elaine of Martin Ellis's death, the ultimate in horror that the man she had once promised to marry had pursued her over a rooftop with a gun, intent on murdering her and died, his bones smashed, at her feet. His most profound hope was that he'd learn before he drove her home, but knowing her closed and secretive nature he wasn't optimistic.

She was waiting in the hall when he rang the bell, dressed in a classic black silk coat over a light dress. That there was no open sign of grief on her face, lifted his heart. "Why, you're ready!"

"You can be late for a play or a film and get away with it, but be late for a symphony concert in Coldbridge and you run the risk of being hissed or glared at by the conductor."

He wanted to ask her how she was but his courage was sapped by the nagging fear that the ill-chosen word, the wrong gesture would drive her farther from him. Anyway, for the moment, it was enough that, physically, she looked in good shape.

It was only when they'd discussed the concert, ordered their meal, and were sipping their drinks, that he asked: "Elaine, how are you? I want to know."

She hesitated, her glance first seeking his, then flicking away. "I suppose you could say I'm in the process of finding out. I've made a beginning by telling Kenneth I'm leaving. It threw him badly—the desertion of the oldest of old faithfuls!" She sipped, added: "And I'm selling the house and every single thing in it."

"Ghosts put behind you! Banished forever. Bravo!"

She smiled tentatively. "Thank you for not saying about time! That I'm years too late."

"You're not too late for anything," he said, feeling his way, and when she did not reply, felt a pinch of alarm. "Then what?"

"I've an old school friend. For a while, until she got married, we worked side by side at Robson & Bates. Her husband is in the British Consulate in Paris. When . . ." She stumbled, went on in a rush: "When it all happened she telephoned me, and I promised to go and stay with them in Neuilly. They have a baby girl, Charlotte Elaine, who is my goddaughter although I've never seen her."

"I'm glad," he said, not knowing whether he was or he wasn't. "Just what you need. You might even settle in Paris for a while."

"No. I'll spend a couple of weeks with Mary and then I'll probably go on to Italy." A luminosity came into her eyes. "To Tuscany, to see the villages that cling so tightly to the tops of the hills that, in the pictures, they look part of them. Everyone has some special place they long to see. Mine's Sienna." For a moment she dreamed silently, with that curious, lovely look of innocence she never wholly lost. "After that I might go on to Sicily."

He had to work hard to smile encouragement. "You could sail from Palermo to North Africa."

She shook her head. "You're forgetting Rosie's wedding. I have to be back by late December. Then in the new year, before idling becomes an ingrained habit, I'll shop around for a new job. Probably in London." She broke off, her expression puzzled. "Why the grin?"

"You wouldn't know how much of a kick I get out of thinking of us both in London."

She said nothing, looking away from him into the middle-distance. It was a laugh that deflected it, a woman's laugh, spontaneous and huskily joyous. She was in an alcove, copper hair spotlighted by the down-beam of a wall-mounted candlelight, bending forward, until their faces were only a couple of inches apart, towards a blond man, whose answering laugh was crisper and more incisive. That red hair—speculation struck and as quickly faded away. Dozens, maybe a hundred, redheads in Coldbridge, and the distance had been too long for her to see the features distinctly. In the end all she felt was a whisper of envy for a spectacular-looking couple who were simply, with no visible complexities, relishing every moment of each other's company.

Robert, watching her, drew in his breath, held it and then let it out slowly. "Elaine, I've got to ask, if not now at some time in the future; avoiding the issue turns it into a pit into which one of us will fall. Did you love him? Tell me honestly, did you?"

She took her glance from the couple in the alcove, and instantly he was conscious of the open play of emotion on her face: memory, sorrow, pity and something deeper, like repentance, but repentance for what—loving or not loving?

When at last she spoke it was with quiet steadfastness, as though she were determinedly making a confession. "People don't believe that a child can fall in love. But it happens. I know, because it happened to me. Martin's parents literally idolised him; maybe I caught their idolatry, like an infectious disease. And because I was so young, the love grew with me, so much a part of me I couldn't have torn it out even if I'd wanted to. Martin accepted it as his right. Mainly because it bought him favours from his mother who'd been scheming towards one end since we were in our early teens. Though she'd never have admitted it, she was agonisingly aware of his weaknesses, the cracks in his character: that he'd lie, cheat, steal to get money or win an advantage over someone else. She believed—no, I'm sure she prayed—that I'd protect him when she was dead, be a wife who'd provide him with a safety net from himself." She smiled ironically. "And me? The simple answer is I saw myself as his saviour."

He protested: "But when he left Coldbridge, bolted, then surely . . ."

"Even that didn't cure me. I'd fret nights away afraid he'd lie and be found out, or steal and be caught. Without me, I imagined him ending up in some filthy gaol in another continent. Sheer conceit!" She paused, finished: "Also I was sure that one day, when his parents were dead, that the house, the money they left, would pull him back to Coldbridge, and that we'd meet again."

"He came back as a killer. You had in your possession

a piece of evidence which you deliberately kept from the police. For God's sake, why? The answer can only be that you loved him."

"No, love isn't the right word. Perhaps bondage, a self-imposed enslavement. I don't know. I honestly don't."

Her face became remote as her flesh re-experienced in the warmth of the hotel dining room the claylike coldness, the freezing of the heart as though it were being slowly enclosed in ice, she'd suffered that Sunday morning. But how to convey to anyone else the shocking, utterly terrorising suspicion that had gripped her in that bloodied room? Yet heart and mind longed to do so, as though it were a gateway to sunlight that would open if she had sufficient courage to walk towards it. She closed her eyes as a shield against his expression of horror or derision as she spoke. "It wasn't the pen. That was mass-produced; it could have been dropped by anyone with those initials, and I held on to it so long, twirling it round that the only fingerprints on it would have been mine. No, it was something else, eerie beyond description. It was as though his presence in that room and what he did there had left an imprint that only I could see, like a photograph of a segment of the past."

She opened her eyes, and his look of horrified incredulity drove her to jeer fiercely at herself. "What does that make me! It sounds like a chapter from a spooky Victorian novelette. Either that or I'm crazy." She looked around her like a scared child. "Maybe I am, and that's the whole answer."

"You're not," he said with deadly conviction. "Elaine, you're not. Don't even think it, not for a single moment."

She shook her head slowly. "Now, at this minute I don't begin to understand that Sunday morning. It's no more than a nightmare I once had, but at the time it was so real to me, a three-dimensional picture in my mind that I couldn't concentrate on anything but, somehow, finding out if it was true."

"And you did." To ease the tension that crippled them both, he resorted to a rough and ready summing-up of the

182

case. "Though even if you hadn't, the police, admittedly late in the day, were on to him. They brought an old man from Cornwall, who'd shown Ellis a newspaper with an account of his father's death, and he'd denied knowing him. Presumably with the idea of fogging the issue, he'd cooked up this woolly scheme of what amounted to hiding out for the best part of a week after he'd murdered his father. In the end, it wouldn't have saved him but, to a degree, it protected him from the initial heat, gave him time to dispose of the weapon, and blood-stained clothing. Even so, very curious, wholly pointless, like a scared child hiding away in a cupboard after he's raided the fridge. Also the police had made investigations into the pending hotel deal and discovered that Ellis had no more than a few hundred pounds to his name, and no earthly hope of producing the £7,500 that the hotel owner was demanding. And lastly, a guest who'd been on his way to the bathroom at 5 A.M. on Sunday morning, three hours later than Ellis claimed he'd arrived back at the hotel, had seen him stealing into his bedroom wearing a soddened raincoat."

She nodded her head in acknowledgment, but he doubted whether she had taken in his words. Then, without warning, the shadows lifted from her eyes, and she said with warmth designed to comfort him: "I don't expect anyone to understand, not even you, when I hardly do myself. Please, don't worry."

He saw the two houses, the occupants of which looked into each other's front windows. In one a mourning widower, suddenly burdened with the task of bringing up a five-year-old girl. In the other a dominant, ferociously possessive mother-figure, hatching dreams to protect a weakling son from himself. And in between, at their mercy, a girl and a boy. Two average, impeccably respectable middle-class homes—except one had become a forcing ground for murder.

He said in his gentlest voice: "Maybe you're right, and I don't understand, except to a limited extent. It's a situation that has to be lived over years. Lived in the heart." He lightened his tone. "Eat your supper. And remember we have a date at Rosie's wedding."

He raised his glass, and after a pause she, almost shyly, raised hers.

As they drank, he wondered if he'd wait for her in vain, or alternatively get tired of waiting. Then, inexplicably, catching her glance that was suddenly and miraculously washed clean of tension and secrecy, hope blazed, became conviction, and he could have laughed aloud with joy. Patience, my boy, he schooled himself, that's what you must cultivate.